GUARDIANS
of GA'HOOLE

A Guide Book to the
Great Tree

✦ OTULISSA ✦

GUARDIANS
of GA'HOOLE

A Guide Book to the Great Tree

BY OTULISSA,
A GUARDIAN OF THE GREAT TREE
With the Most Essential Guidance of Kathryn Huang

SCHOLASTIC INC.

New York   Toronto   London   Auckland
Sydney   Mexico City   New Delhi   Hong Kong

No part of this publication may be reproduced, stored in a retrieval system, or transmitted in any form or by any means, electronic, mechanical, photocopying, recording, or otherwise, without written permission of the publisher. For information regarding permission, write to Scholastic Inc., Attention: Permissions Department, 557 Broadway, New York, NY 10012.

ISBN 978-0-439-93188-5

Text copyright © 2007 by Kathryn Lasky
and Kathryn Huang Knight

Illustrations copyright © 2007 by Scholastic Inc. All rights reserved. Published by Scholastic Inc. SCHOLASTIC and associated logos are trademarks and/or registered trademarks of Scholastic Inc.

Design by Steve Scott

Illustrated by Richard Cowdrey

12 11 10 9 8 7 6 5   12 13 14 15 16/0

Printed in the U.S.A.   23

First printing, October 2007

Containing ...

First, a Word . . .

Attention, scholars of Ga'Hoole! You know the Great Ga'Hoole Tree as the home of honor and benevolence, of scholarship and invention, and above all, the home of an order of knightly owls known as the Guardians of Ga'Hoole.

It is a historic time at the tree. Boron, Barran, Strix Struma, and Ezylryb have all passed into glaumora. The arrival of Coryn, the first true king in a millennium, is bringing about an era of monumental change. We, the new generation of Guardians, have inherited the great tree, and there is much for us to do. This is a pivotal time, as was the time of the legends, and it must be remembered. This is why I, Otulissa, have written this volume. It is my hope that future generations of Ga'Hoolian scholars will read this and understand what life was like at the great tree during our time. With that, I give you A Guide Book to the Great Tree.

The Natural (and Supernatural) History of the Great Ga'Hoole Tree

The Great Ga'Hoole Tree stands alone on the Island of Hoole in the Sea of Hoolemere, a symbol of goodness and nobility, a place of selfless deeds and heroism. Above all, it is my home. And I love it, with my heart and my gizzard.

"Ga'Hoole" means the "Great Spirit of Hoole" — a befitting name. In the time of the legends, as Hoole and his companions approached the island, the scores of owls that followed them cried out, "The Great Ga'Hoole Tree! The Great Ga'Hoole Tree!" And so the name would forever be remembered in the annals of history.

Ours is the first and largest tree of its kind. It rises hundreds of feet into the air. It would take one hundred of the largest Great Gray Owls, with their wings fully stretched, to surround the enormous trunk. Its branches reach out in every direction over the Sea of Hoolemere, giving the tree a glorious green crown in the times of the Silver Rain and Golden Rain. During the time of the Copper-Rose Rain, the leaves turn to varying shades of gold and russet.

Massive in form, and perfect in symmetry, the Great Ga'Hoole Tree can be confused with none other. Its roots reach to the farthest edges of the island. Strix Pycelle, a botanist in the time of Hoole, documented that the root of any tree beneath the Earth's surface is as big as the tree itself aboveground. Imagine, then, a mass of roots burrowing hundreds of feet deep, anchoring our home in the sky above. From a distance, the trunk and limbs of the great tree shimmer in the light of the setting sun. This is because the tree develops knobby bark in shades of brown in the times of the Golden Rain and Copper-Rose Rain, and smooth white bark in the times of White Rain and Silver Rain. New shoots have a bright red tint. All the colors, when combined with the reflections from the sea, give the great tree a scintillating presence.

The Great Ga'Hoole Tree wasn't always the giant you see today. It began, as all trees do, as a seed. Some find it astonishing that a seed could have even reached the island given the great distance it had to travel over the Sea of Hoolemere. Maybe it was carried by a great gust of wind, or stowed away in the feathers of an unknowing bird — nobody truly understands how it got here. Nonetheless, the seed found itself on this once-barren island. I can only guess that the beginning of our great tree was somewhat . . . magical in nature.

One legend claims it was King Hoole who caused the seedling to burst forth from the ground; that he unwittingly imbued the seed with Ga as he and his companion, Grank, flew over the then-barren island. Grank himself thought that it was Hoole's tears, tears he shed for his mother, Siv, that caused the seed to sprout. Others say it was the great ember that summoned the sleepy seedling to wake from afar in anticipation of the coming of the true king. In any case, the seedling grew at an astounding rate. Young Hoole himself saw the seedling grow to the height of his best friend, Phineas, before his very eyes.

Soon after King Hoole established the Guardians of Ga'Hoole in the great tree in the time of the legends, the great tree was put on record as being "hundreds" of feet high — an astonishing fact, as even the fastest-growing trees only grow six to seven feet a year. It is roughly one thousand years old.

The tree developed many comfortable hollows for all its new residents. This, too, must have been supernatural, for it cannot be explained by science; most trees don't have hollows until they have reached middle age at two to three hundred years old. According to the annals, the tree seemed to understand the needs of its owl inhabitants. The hollows accommodated just the right number of owls. There were big hollows for the likes of Great Grays; small, cozy ones for Elf and Pygmy owls; and every size in between. The Great Hollow has always been there, ready to serve whatever needs the Guardians had. So, too, has the hollow that became parliament. Hoole chose this particular hollow because it was closest to the roots of the great tree. He did this to remind us that the source of the Guardians' power is rooted in earthly values — goodness, equality, and nobility of deed. So it seems that the tree has always recognized its purpose, and ours.

Another curious phenomenon observed by all the owls of Ga'Hoole is the perennial thick fog that hovers over the island. According to the legends, in the instant that Hoole and his companions flew over our island for the first time, the clouds parted in the sky, and the fog lifted from the sea. A beam of moonlight guided them to the tree. It was as if Glaux had opened a great gate over the island. Strix Estera, a little-known, but nonetheless respected weathertrix of the Age of Enlightenment, concluded that the great spirit of the tree summons this fog to protect its inhabitants from unwanted intruders. Mist conceals the island, parting only for those deemed worthy. Those unfamiliar with the location of our island often fly right over it without ever knowing what rises up beneath them. However, this protection is not foolproof. The so-called Pure Ones, led by Kludd, were able to penetrate the mist when they launched their attack upon the Great Ga'Hoole Tree — a terrible episode known simply as the Siege.

It might surprise some to know that the great tree has lived for a thousand years without ever coming to any lasting harm. After much research, this writer found only two incidences in the history of the tree when the Guardians thought the tree was in danger of permanent injury — or death.

The first such incident occurred early within the Age of Enlightenment. The Ga'Hoolologist at that time was a young Barn Owl named Sianna. She noticed one spring night that the great tree had a new guest, a caterpillar that glowed with all the colors of the rainbow. Caterpillars are a common sight on the great tree and make a tasty snack. But this one was different. Not only was it beautiful, unlike other caterpillars, it also spun fine, multicolored globules of silk that hung between branches like large teardrops, mimicking the shape of our prized milkberries. The silken teardrops were glorious to behold. They sparkled and twirled in the moonlight. The colors constantly shifted, creating mysterious shapes on the surface of the silk. It was said that once you looked upon one, it was most difficult to look away. The owls called them luminaspheres.

Sianna, along with many other owls of the great tree, was mesmerized. The rainbow caterpillars were declared a blessing from Glaux that glorified the Great Ga'Hoole Tree. It was proclaimed that no owl should eat any of these caterpillars. Inhabitants of the great tree would spend several hours each night admiring the luminaspheres that covered the tree, sometimes neglecting their other duties.

Unbeknownst to the distracted owls, hidden from view by the luminaspheres, the rainbow caterpillars were devouring the leaves and new shoots of the Great Ga'Hoole Tree, stunting its growth. The tree was suffering. This went on for weeks, then months.

As the time passed, Heilo the Blind, an old Spotted Owl and retired weather interpretation ryb, began to get odd twinges in his gizzard. Unable to see the luminaspheres, Heilo was immune to their bewitching effects. He couldn't put his talon on it, but he knew something was very wrong. He shut himself in his hollow for a period of intense and undisturbed meditation, and finally sensed the true nature of the tree's sickness. At once he knew the cause. Despite Sianna's protests, he informed the parliament, which ordered the destruction of all luminaspheres and the death of all the rainbow caterpillars. And so it was done.

Later that year, the milkberry harvest was paltry. The berries that did grow were small and tasted chalky. It would be three years before the tree fully recovered. The owls learned a valuable lesson, and Heilo the Blind was hailed as a hero. Since that time, the great tree has been tended to with much vigilance to ensure that it remains free from unfriendly visitors.

The second incident occurred only a few centuries ago. During one particularly damp period in the season of the Golden Rain, it was noted in the annals that the Great Ga'Hoole Tree did not grow as profuse a green crown as it had during previous years. Its leaves looked small and sickly, and its branches sagged under an invisible weight.

The famed Ga'Hoolologist and ryb Isolde, a Burrowing Owl, set out to find the cause. She and the Ga'Hoolology chaw flittered through the boughs, examined the colossal trunk, and poked around the roots. It was no easy task, surveying the great tree. (It must have been mind-numbingly boring, too. Why, I'd rather bury pellets.) After several days and several inspections, Isolde found the first clue.

Black fire mushrooms

Little mushrooms of a kind Isolde had never before seen were growing in a crack near the roots. They had ominous matte-black caps shaped like clamshells, and thick yellow stalks. When Isolde touched the caps with her wing tips, a fine black powder spurted from them into the air. On a moonless night, she cut into the root beneath the mushrooms with the aid of a pair of modified battle claws. To her horror and amazement, she discovered streaks within the heartwood of the root that glowed like fire in the night. With the color and intensity of hot coals from the forge, the streaks lit up Isolde's face. She

9

cut along the root farther into the ground, and discovered that the streaks ran deep into the tree, zigzagging, she was certain, through much of the root system.

The Ga'Hoolology chaw had never seen anything like this before. Several young owls in the chaw were transfixed at the sight; some muttered that the streaks were the result of nachtmagen. A mood of both enchantment and fear spread through the group.

The next night, Isolde and her chaw set out to find a cure for the great tree. The chaw split up into pairs and flew to various parts of the Southern Kingdoms, seeking knowledge from all the sage creatures of the land. Pollianne the Barn Owl and Hildeth the Spotted Owl headed for the Shadow Forest to seek an old Snowy named Aude who had a reputation as a tree healer. Elva the Elf Owl and Sanders, another Barn Owl, went to the Forest of Tyto in search of the Dark Sisters, a group of nest-maid snakes who were masters of potions and poultices. Isolde and Marduk, a Great Gray, headed for the Forest of Ambala to speak with the eagles, who always seemed to know the latest happenings in the entire kingdom. The three groups would reconvene in Ambala to discuss their findings.

Elva and Sanders found the Dark Sisters in a hollow of an oak tree formerly inhabited by a family of Great Grays. "We can give you what you seek, if you know what you

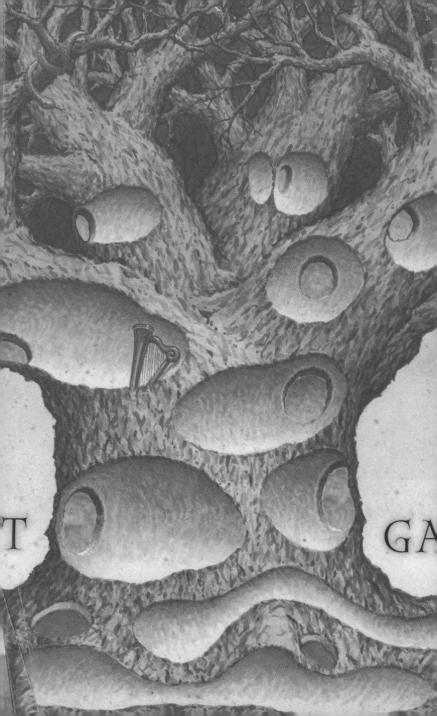

THOOLE TREE
A Through-the-Bark View

seek," the blind snakes said. Elva and Sanders tried to explain the glowing streaks in the root of the Great Ga'Hoole Tree, but without knowing the name of the condition, the Sisters could not concoct a cure. Thwarted, the two young owls flew onward to Ambala to reconvene with the rest of the chaw.

Aude the Snowy did not disappoint. He knew at once the name and nature of the malady. To Hildeth and Polianne he uttered two words: "black fire." A nasty thing black fire was. When it got into a young tree's roots, it could kill the tree within a year. A stronger, older tree could live with black fire for several years before it died, but die it would, and a vile end it would have. Black fire had not been seen in the Southern Kingdoms in hundreds of years, Aude had claimed. But the glowing streaks in the heartwood of the roots could mean nothing else.

"There is a cure, a potion made from an herb called Lyssop," Aude told Polianne and Hildeth. "But I have none of it, and I have not seen it in these parts since I was a mere owlet." Polianne and Hildeth rushed this news to Ambala.

In the Forest of Ambala, the eagles reported that several stands of trees in Ambala had been killed in the last year by a yet unknown malady. It was now clear — black fire was back in the Southern Kingdoms.

Armed with the information brought back by Polianne

and Hildeth, Isolde and the Ga'Hoolology chaw once again called on the Dark Sisters.

"Lyssop you seek, Lyssop you shall have," the Sisters chanted. With that, they slithered from their hollow onto the forest floor. "Return in two days," they told the six owls.

And so they waited. When they returned, they were presented with a bottle of bright green liquid. "You must keep the afflicted roots moist with this," the Sisters instructed. "Two weeks, and the herb shall do its work." Isolde held the cure in her talons and gave the Dark Sisters her gratitude.

Back at the Great Ga'Hoole Tree, the Ga'Hoolology chaw went to work. Night and day, the owls took turns moistening the roots with a feather dipped in Lyssop potion. They did this for two weeks, just as the Dark Sisters had said. First, the fiery streaks stopped glowing, and turned an ashen shade of gray. Then, the black mushrooms withered and died. And finally, just as the potion was about to run out, the streaks disappeared, leaving thin hollow channels where they once had glowed.

With the help of the Dark Sisters, black fire was eventually eliminated from all of the Southern Kingdoms. But, if it came once, it could come again. For this reason I always include both the disease and the cure in my teachings.

Something struck me the last time I taught my black fire lesson to my chaw. I have looked at Isolde's diagrams again and again. Only this time I noticed the location of the affected areas of the roots. The black fire started at the northeast side of the tree and burrowed inward. Why, it must have passed right under the parliamentary hollow. Is it possible that a case of black fire several hundred years ago allowed certain owls, who will remain unnamed, to overhear what was being said in the parliamentary hollow? Oh, to think of it!

It might seem improper to have such information in a book of this nature. But our little listening station is a feature of the tree, and it must be recorded for posterity.

Even though the Great Ga'Hoole Tree has lived about a thousand years, it continues to grow and change. We understand now that we must care for the great tree, as it cares for us. We tend to its needs as it tends to ours. It is my job as the Ga'Hoolology ryb to teach all the young owls the importance of tending to our living home.

I should mention that although I was never in the Ga'Hoolology chaw, I am, in fact, the current

Ga'Hoolology ryb. After the, well — how shall I put it? — less-than-voluntary departure of Dewlap, the tree was in dire need of a new Ga'Hoolology ryb. Thanks to that boring old Burrowing Owl, the subject was seen by all students as the most tedious of the whole tree. As much as I hated the endless hours of pellet-burying as a young owl, I knew the importance of caring for our home. I saw an opportunity for a change. So, I volunteered to fill the post of Ga'Hoolology ryb, determined to ignite a passion for learning about our beloved tree in my young charges. It's true that I was double-chawed in weather interpretation and colliering; nevertheless, I had always made it a point to be proficient in all subjects. I am still learning about the subject, of course. But I hope that I have made Ga'Hoolology a more exciting subject for young students.

Ember holder

With that, I will end my treatise on the natural history of the Great Ga'Hoole Tree. According to the legends, the awesome powers of the Ember of Hoole remained on the island while Hoole ruled here. Some believed it was the ember that made the tree great. But King Hoole knew better. He realized that, although the great tree had magical beginnings, the power of the tree was rooted in the collective spirit of the Guardians. It is the principles of honor, virtue, and the pursuit of knowledge that give the great tree its power. So, since the time of Hoole, those principles have guided us. The tree and the Guardians have needed no magic to thrive.

May both flourish for ages to come.

The Making of a Guardian

Honor, virtue, kindness, purity of heart . . . of course, these are all ingredients that go into the making of a Guardian of Ga'Hoole. But becoming a Guardian requires, beyond all the intangible qualities, a proper education.

When Hoole founded our great tree, he realized that there was an infinite number of things to be taught and learned, and that this learning, beyond all the magen in the world, would make the tree great. And so, he introduced unto owlkind the "chaw" as we know it. During King H'rathmore's reign in ancient times, owls came together for sport, to practice their fighting skills, and for general learning, in small groups called chaws. The chaws of today come together in much the same way, to hone skills and pass on knowledge to any owl who wishes to learn, regardless of species or background, but today the scope of our teaching is much broader. For those of you not yet fortunate to be in study at the great tree, I have listed some of the courses now taught here.

CHAW FUNDAMENTALS

All young owls of the tree begin their education with Chaw Fundamentals. These classes are required, and must be completed before owls are chosen for a chaw. The material taught in these classes is general, but of utmost importance; it is knowledge that every chaw member should have. Plus, owls are introduced to a wealth of tools that become indispensable later in their lives. In fact, it was in Chaw Fundamentals that I first encountered a book by my illustrious ancestor, the renowned weathertrix Strix Emerilla.

Now that I am a ryb (even though I have chosen to dispense with the title in day-to-day life, like many others before me), I get such joy from seeing owlets learn new skills for the first time. Oh, to be young again . . . to be so open to possibilities. In these pre-chaw assignment classes, young owls get a chance to figure out which chaws they might like best and in which chaw their own unique talents best fit, while the rybs scout out those who show special talent for their own chaws. Sometimes, an owl knows right away in her gizzard which chaw is right for her. Other times, an owl's calling takes him by surprise. I remember when I, along with the Band, was about to be chaw tapped. Twilight knew from the start that he was perfect for search-and-rescue, and sure enough, that's the chaw that he was tapped for. I, on the other hand, thought for sure that I would be tapped for the Navigation Chaw. Oh, how I absolutely, positively, categorically adored my navigation classes with Strix Struma. Instead, I was double chawed in colliering and weather interpretation. It was a disappointment. To be perfectly frank, I was frinked off for quite a while about that one. But, it all worked out for the best in the end. I know now that I was meant for those chaws, and I couldn't have made a better choice myself.

Remedial Flight Lab and Power Flight
(For Weak Fliers Only)
Taught by the distinguished ryb Poot
All newly arrived young owls to the great tree must be evaluated by a team of rybs for flight proficiency. Those deemed weak fliers will be required to attend remedial flight lab. This course teaches the fundamentals of sound flight, basic flapping, upstrokes, downstrokes, power liftoff, wing control, air carving, basic steering, and flying

information. After three sessions, owls are reevaluated for fitness to move on to other coursework.

Beginner Search-and-Rescue Techniques
Taught by the distinguished ryb Twilight
Strong flight skills are crucial to search-and-rescue efforts. This course will teach advanced flying skills, including effective high-altitude and low-altitude circling, diving, emergency landings, and in-flight object retrieval. Owls will go on real reconnaissance missions and deliver oral and written reports to their classmates. Partner work will also be covered, as all search-and-rescue operations require owls to work in pairs. With the ryb's approval, some owls will be introduced to battle claws, and be taught how to fly with them.

Winds and Things
Taught by the distinguished ryb Ruby
Wind and flight are intricately linked. Knowing how to fly in different types of wind and how to use wind to one's advantage are two things that set the owls of the Great Ga'Hoole Tree apart from other owls. In this class, owls will be taught to fly in turbulent winds and harsh weather conditions. The structure of a storm, including thermals (warm updrafts), gutters (the main trough of air in a strong

wind), scuppers (where the edge of the winds of gutters spill over), swillages (where scuppers meet still air), and baggywrinkles (the shredded air currents that lie between the scuppers and the gutter) will be covered. Everyone in this class will be required to fly in at least one small storm.

Introductory Celestial Navigation
Taught by the distinguished ryb Gylfie

In this class, owls will be taught to look to the sky to plot their course of travel. Students will be asked to recognize key stars and constellations in the Hoolemere region, and how they relate to landmass locations at different times of the year. The course will present opportunities to go on as many night flights as possible. Owls will also fly with the navigation chaw for observation and to participate in simple tracing exercises.

Basic Care and Maintenance of the Great Tree
Taught by the distinguished ryb Otulissa

The Great Ga'Hoole Tree has been home to hundreds of thousands of owls during the last millennium. It is our duty as Guardians to make sure it continues to thrive. In this course, owls will learn how to maintain a symbiotic relationship with the tree. A significant part of the course will be devoted to practical exercises, including pellet-burying, vine-trimming, and pruning. Each owl will also be required to write two essays, and pop quizzes will be given at the ryb's discretion.

Common Metals and Their Uses
Taught by the distinguished ryb Bubo

The Guardians depend on various types of metals in their day-to-day activities. This course will introduce young owls to the metals that can easily be found on or near the Island of Hoole. Books used in this course will include: *How to Identify Metals*; *Elemental Metals in the Southern Kingdoms*; *Mu Metal and Its Implications for Magnetics*; and *Metal-Shaping with Fire*. Owls will also be introduced to the forge. There, they will be asked to identify the basic tools used by blacksmiths. At the end of the course, owls will take the F.A.S.T. (Forge Acumen and Safety Test). Those who pass will receive their Forge Safety Certificate and be allowed to begin work at the forge.

Tracking Birds and Small Land Animals
Taught by the distinguished ryb Sylvanna

All animals, including owls, leave tracks. Events are almost always recorded in the tracks of an animal. Tracks can tell you a lot about an animal: where it was headed, its speed of travel, even its size, health, and age. This course will teach owls how to identify the tracks of birds and small land animals, and how to piece together clues that tell us about an event that occurred in the past. Owls in this class will work with the tracking chaw on tactical tracking operations to develop proper groundwork skills.

The Lives of Forest Fires
Taught by the distinguished ryb Elvan

Once categorically feared by creatures of the forest, wildfires are now considered both friend and foe to owlkind. Studying forest fires is crucial to harnessing their power. In this class, owls will take the first step in the study of colliering. We will learn about the elements of a fire, how forest fires start, the properties of thermal drafts, coal types and their formation, and fuel ladders. Different types of fires — crawling, crown, jumping, and smoldering — will be covered and observed, opportunities permitting, of course. At the end of the course, all owls will be ready for fire penetration and coal retrieval.

ADVANCED CHAW PRACTICE

Once an owl is tapped for a chaw, his or her study intensifies. It then becomes the owl's mission to master the chosen field. Those of us who have a proclivity for hard work and scholarship (I shall name no names) may even choose to branch out and master other fields as well. I cannot imagine a better place to pursue an education than at the great tree. Here is just a small sampling of the subjects that can be studied.

Owl Studies: Gizzard Matters

(Open to All Chaws)

Taught by the distinguished ryb Soren

"The gizzard is a marvelous organ . . ." So begins the classic volume *Tempers of the Gizzard: An Interpretative Physiology of This Vital Organ in Strigiformes.* Never have truer words been written. We owls attribute our most profound feelings to the gizzard. Therefore, it makes a fascinating subject of study. In this course, we will take an abstract approach beyond physical processes in studying the nature of the gizzard and how it guides us. We will attempt to answer the question — what can we feel with our gizzards? How do we use our gizzards in various decision-making processes? Can gizzards be more reliable than logic? And, how can we further develop our gizzuition? We will also cover disorders of the gizzard and the effects of flecks, moon blinking, moon scalding, and shattering.

The Natural History of the Great Tree
(Ga'Hoolology Chaw)
Taught by the distinguished ryb Otulissa
The Great Ga'Hoole Tree is a most unusual tree. Beyond its immense size and extraordinary longevity, its natural history is full of fascinating facts and phenomena. By learning about its intriguing past we can ensure that it will have a healthy future. In this course, we will study the growth patterns of the tree, the various blights and tree diseases that it has suffered, and how the actions of its inhabitants have affected it.

Advanced Battle-Claw Fighting Techniques
(Search-and-Rescue Chaw)
Taught by the distinguished ryb Twilight
Once owls can comfortably and reliably fly while wearing battle claws, they can go on to learn more advanced fighting techniques. The art of the battle claw is highly intuitive, but there is much that can be learned and perfected. We will cover all defensive and offensive maneuvers including slashing, blocking, diving thrusts, reverse shears, and

two-footed attacks. The drawbacks of fighting with battle claws will be covered in depth, as will methods of clawless defense against a battle-clawed opponent.

Ga'Hoolian History
(Open to All Chaws)
Taught by the distinguished ryb Otulissa
This course traces Ga'Hoole's social, political, and cultural development from the founding of the tree through the arrival of the new king. Key topics include the rise of Hoole, the effects of the ember at the great tree, the Gray Ages, the Northern Alliance, the War of the Ice Claws, the Battle of Little Hoole, and the rise and fall of the Pure Ones. Among other texts, the Legends of Ga'Hoole will be closely studied.

Fire and Ice Weapons
(Open to All Chaws)
Taught by the distinguished rybs Twilight and Ruby
Ice weapons have been used by owls since before the time of the legends. Fire weapons were recently developed in battle by the Guardians of Ga'Hoole. Used in conjunction with battle claws, fire and ice weapons present a most lethal combination. However, both require intensive training to master. In this course, owls who have proven their

proficiency in fighting with battle claws will learn to wield the ice weapon and fire weapon appropriate for their size and skill level. For the ice weapons portion of the course, smaller owls will be taught the deadly art of the ice splinter — a weapon that requires blistering speed and pinpoint precision. Larger owls will be taught to use ice swords and ice scimitars. All owls will be required to learn the procedures of ice harvesting, blade honing, and proper weapons storage and preservation. For the fire weapons portion of the course, owls will be required to study thermal disturbances, efficient branch ignition, and how wind patterns affect combustion. Owls will also be taught group attack strategies when flying with flaming branches.

Ice scimitar

Owl Studies: The Healing Arts
(Open to All Chaws)
Taught by the distinguished ryb Westley

From the founding of the great tree, the Guardians of Ga'Hoole have been committed to helping the sick and injured. This course will introduce owls to the healing arts that have been practiced here for centuries. Topics covered include owl physiology, the proper use of worms and leeches, the history of major owl plagues in the Northern and Southern kingdoms, and the preparation of potions and poultices. After four lectures, owls will work as interns in the infirmary hollow, in close conjunction with nest-maid snakes.

Blacksmithing
(Metals Chaw, Also Open to Colliering Chaw)
Taught by the distinguished ryb Bubo
Owls who have received their Forge Safety Certificate can formally begin their study in the art of blacksmithing. At the forge, students will be referred to as apprentices. This is not one of those bookish courses; all learning here is talons-on. Apprentices will learn to identify bonk coals, build and maintain forge fires, and correctly use hammer and tongs. At the end of the course, students should be able to make simple objects such as buckets and bowls.

Hurricanes, Tornadoes, and Other Weather Phenomena
(Weather-Interpretation Chaw)
Taught by the distinguished ryb Ruby
The weather-interpretation chaw is ready to fly in any condition, no matter how dangerous. But we never fly

into storms blindly, we always know our enemy before we engage. By using our brains, as well as our wings, we can learn to fly safely in all sorts of foul weather. With any luck, we will fly, as a chaw, through thunderstorms, hurricanes, tornadoes, blizzards, hailstorms, and even sandstorms. Owls in this course must always be ready to fly at a moment's notice.

Independent Study and Exchange Program
(Open to All Chaws)

The rybs of the great tree promote the pursuit of knowledge beyond what's offered at the tree. Therefore, we offer an exchange program with the Glauxian Brothers' retreat in the Bitter Sea. The Glauxian Brothers are masters in the healing arts, as well as in bookmaking and poetry. Plus, their library rivals ours at the great tree. Guardians are encouraged to spend a season or two studying and meditating with the brothers.

THE GUARDIAN'S OATH

Most owls spend several years in chaw studies before they are welcomed into the brotherhood of the Guardians. When an owl is deemed ready, he or she takes owlkind's most inviolable oath: the Oath of the Guardians. I took this oath on a crisp autumn night in the company of kindred spirits. As I repeated these words after Barran, the great Snowy Owl and then steward of the tree, they became forever etched in my heart and my gizzard.

I am a Guardian of Ga'Hoole. From this night on, I dedicate my life to the protection of owlkind. I shall not swerve in my duty. I shall support my brother and sister Guardians in times of battle as well as in times of peace. I am the eyes in the night, the silence within the wind. I am the talons through the fire, the shield that guards the innocent. I shall seek to wear no crown, nor win any glory. And all these things I do swear upon my honor as a Guardian of Ga'Hoole until my days on this Earth cease to be. This be my vow. This be my life. By Glaux I do swear.

The Faces of the Great Tree

Scholars of Ga'Hoole, you know well the tales of Soren, of our new king, Coryn, and of our revered founder, Hoole. What you may not know is that there are multitudes of owls from the Great Ga'Hoole Tree whose stories remain untold. Theirs are the stories that will show you what the tree truly represents. No legends celebrate their deeds, yet they are heroes, many, and scoundrels, some, without whose stories the history of the tree is incomplete. I present to you just a few of these stories.

TWILIGHT

It is undeniable that Twilight is a force unto himself. He is a member of the Band and of the Chaw of Chaws, a fierce fighter, a powerful flier, an expressive poet, a notorious braggart, and a loyal friend. So, what more needs to be said about this Great Gray? Oh, you might be surprised to know what I have learned.

✾ TWILIGHT ✾

Many of us owls at the great tree are orphans, myself included. What sets Twilight apart is that he was orphaned at a very young age, possibly within a day of being hatched. He has no memories of his family or his nest. All he knows is that he was hatched at the edges of time. Most owlets would have died, but Twilight survived. Twilight *is* a survivor. Twilight has lived in every kingdom in the south and with every kind of creature. He was taken in by a family of woodpeckers in Ambala, an elderly eagle in Tyto, and even a family of desert foxes in Kuneer. He has also lived alone, drifting from one place to another, without the companionship and support of family or friends. All his experiences have made him tougher, but also more compassionate and more open-minded. When Twilight came to the tree, he had no memory of family, no idea where he came from. And even though he doesn't let on, I know that it has always weighed heavily on his mind.

Things took a curious turn for Twilight one night shortly after the Battle of the Burning. The Band and I were out for a night flight. We were enjoying some lovely thermal drafts near the edge of Ambala, when Twilight suddenly banked steeply and flew off by himself. He circled the sky in the distance for what seemed like an eternity before Digger decided to go fetch him so we could all go back to the tree together. It was almost Deep

Gray, and the sun would be rising soon. Moments later, the two owls came back toward us in a heated debate.

"No. I'm telling you for the last time, I didn't see any owl," Digger said through clenched beak. "You were the only owl in the sky aside from us."

"How could you not see her?" Twilight demanded. "Um, hello. She was big and gray against a clear night sky." His yellow eyes were huge, and he had puffed himself up to almost twice his usual enormous size.

"Twilight! Get a grip!" Soren chimed in.

"Oh, for Glaux's sake. You guys saw her, didn't you?" Twilight asked.

"Who?"

"That Great Gray. She was flying not fifty pytes from me. And she was trying to tell me something, or ask me something, I know she was. She was right there." Twilight searched the sky desperately with his eyes. Despite being right beside us, he seemed lost. "Didn't you see her? I know she was there."

"Well, I didn't see anything, but maybe I just wasn't paying attention," Gylfie said. She sensed that this was very important to Twilight. This was as pensive as she had ever seen him, and she wasn't about to dismiss his sighting of a phantom owl as a mere optical illusion. "Let's get back to the hollow, and we can talk about it there. Okay, Twi?"

Back in the Band's hollow, we all settled onto perches as the sun rose. (I often joined the Band in their hollow after a night on the wing together.) Twilight continued to look uneasy.

"She was just so . . . I don't know . . . familiar. And then she was gone."

Soren inhaled deeply. His words came out cautiously, "Hmm. Was she all misty? What I mean is, do you think, Twilight, that maybe she was a scroom?"

Scrooms, of course, are the disembodied spirits of owls who have died. Usually, they come back into our world because they have some unfinished business. As young owls, Soren and his sister, Eglantine, had encounters with the scrooms of their parents. So Soren knew firsthand what it was like to be in their presence. Twilight, on the other hand, had never considered himself to be — well, how should I put it — scroomishly inclined.

"What did she say to you?" Soren pushed on.

"Well, it sounded like she said 'cash us'."

"That doesn't make much sense," I told him, a bit too bluntly, now that I think about it.

"Oh, you mean, like 'cache us,' maybe?" Gylfie piped up. "'Cache' means 'to store something away in hiding, especially for later use'."

"Or, it was 'catch.' She was saying, 'catch us!'" I offered. That made a lot more sense to me, but Gylfie shot me an exasperated look.

Digger, the constant theoretician, had another idea. "You can't catch a scroom. That couldn't be it. And who's 'us,' anyway? You said there was only one scroom, right? Maybe she was saying 'cautious.' That you should be cautious. She was warning you about something. You recognized her, you said?"

We all offered other suggestions, but Twilight appeared overwhelmed. "Look, I'm not even saying it *was* a scroom. Maybe it was a reflection or something. . . . I'm not sure about anything anymore. Let's just forget it happened."

But it was clear that Twilight did not forget. For the next few nights, he seemed constantly distracted. He went about chaw practices with uncharacteristic absentmindedness, sometimes even missing his targets during aerial search drills. At mealtimes, we could hardly get more than two words out of him, despite our talk about the newest battle claws that Bubo was working on. I counted eight entire nights without a single chant or song or rhyme from our resident verse-maker. His behavior, his personality was so changed, it was as if the Twilight we knew had disappeared, dissolved like the mist of the scroom that he supposedly saw. Soren, Gylfie, and Digger were clearly worried, and so was I.

During this time, the library of the great tree made some extraordinary acquisitions. I had volunteered to help catalog these precious new finds. I thought it might help to give my gizzard a little lift. And did it ever! Among them were the latest treatises on herbal medicine, an original illuminated manuscript about the Battle of the Ice Palace, and my personal favorite — *Ode: Intimations on Life and Love in the Forest,* a book of contemporary poetry by a *Strix nebulosa* named Skye. Skye was the most notable and celebrated poet of our time; "a prodigy," many learned owls called her. She was said to have disappeared not long ago, and her last book was feared lost. Luckily, a Glauxian Brother found it in an abandoned hollow in the forest of Ambala. The master bookmakers at the retreat made a copy, and, as a gesture of goodwill, gave the Guardians the original.

I immediately checked the book out from the library and began reading. Oh, the poems were lovely and cerebral at the same time, the finest combination, in my opinion! I liked the one called "Moonlight at Midnight" the best, that is, until I read "Elegy for Lone Pine." And, of course, there was "Shall I Fly Into a Storm." I was in glaumora. Needless to say, I finished the entire book in two nights. It was while I was closing the book that I found something intriguing.

Carefully tucked into the lemming leather of the back cover was another poem, written on a folded piece of parchment. I began to read . . .

> *At twilight, you came*
> *so fragile so slight*
> *I gave you your name*
> *Your song I shall write*
>
> *My heart you have won*
> *from the moment you hatched*
> *My precious new son*
> *your worth is unmatched*
>
> *Now it's for you that I sing*
> *my soul filled with pride*
> *To me you can cling*
> *till you can fly alongside*
>
> *I offer you this, my melodic phrase*
> *For you are my most beloved of Grays*

I looked at the title again. My gizzard leaped. I was off at once to gather the Band.

The four of us took shallow, guarded breaths, and watched intently as Twilight read the poem for the fifth, and then sixth time. Bit by bit, it sank in.

"My mum? You mean, this was written by my mum?" He asked all of us and none of us. "This was written by *my mum*." He read the title of the poem aloud one more time, "Ode to My Son Cassius at Twilight."

"Don't you see? The scroom you saw, it was your mum! And she was . . ."

"And she was calling my name," Twilight finished the sentence for Digger. "Cassius. My mum named me Cassius."

I couldn't tell exactly what the Great Gray was feeling at that moment. In his eyes, I saw contentment, confusion, surprise, and a little sadness.

"This must be why I was so drawn to twilight. I think she sang this to me just as I hatched, and all I remembered was the first line. Remember, Soren, when I told you that I knew I was hatched at the edges of time? Well, I think I know now why that was my very first memory.

"It was a family of Pygmy Owls who first took me in as a tiny owlet. Bluebell and Dahlia, mother and daughter. At least, I think Bluebell was the mother, and Dahlia was the daughter. But it could have been the other way around

38

because they only ever referred to each other as 'Big Pyggy' and 'Lil Pyggy.'" Twilight let out a small churr. "They told me that I kept saying the word 'twilight' in my dreams, so they assumed it must have been my name. I quickly outgrew their hollow and moved on. This whole time, I thought it was that silvery border of time between day and night that gave me my name. Cassius. Son of the poet, Skye. Well, go figure."

Twilight had always thought of himself as a plain, down-to-earth sort of owl because he had no proper upbringing. Now, an illustrious heritage was suddenly thrust upon him. Not only was Skye a preeminent poet, but she also had numerous relatives who were well-known writers and artists.

"I don't know . . . I wonder what my mother would have thought of me, if she were alive, I mean. And my aunts and uncles . . . I bet it's not every day they meet a graduate from the Orphan School of Tough Learning. Still, it's as if my gizzard is more whole somehow."

"Your mum loved you, Twi," Digger said softly. "That much is clear."

Twilight acknowledged this with a barely visible nod.

Gylfie finally asked the question that had been on all our minds. "So, what do you want us to call you now? I mean, are you Cassius now?"

The Great Gray who had hatched as Cassius thought for a moment. "My name is Twilight. Now that I know how I got it, it fits me even better. My mum named me Cassius, but in a way, she also named me Twilight. And I think she would be proud of what I've become."

That, no one could disagree with.

Twilight's chest swelled. "I am proud to be the son of Skye, but the world is still my family. You guys are still my family." And with that, he went to the skyport and lifted into the air with one smooth power stroke. Shaking off the malaise of the last days, he raised his voice.

> *We met before moonrise*
> *And then you left, without good-byes*
> *To my rhymes you did give rise*
>
> *Your name I chanced upon*
> *Now you are with me, though you are gone*
> *Our verses shall fly on*

"It's good to have you back, Twilight!" Soren called out.

And indeed it was. You know, that might be my favorite rhyme of his yet.

STRIX STRUMA

No book about the Great Ga'Hoole Tree would be complete without the tale of Strix Struma. She was the venerated navigation ryb and a respected member of parliament for years. Not long ago, she gave her life in defense of the great tree in the fight against the Pure Ones when they besieged us. I fought at her side as a member of Struma's Strikers. She was my mentor and my inspiration, and I loved her well. She shared with me this story as we prepared for battle against the Pure Ones.

The daughter of Strix Hurth, a retired instructor at the Kielian Military Academy, and Strix Otulinn, a respected weathertrix, Struma grew up in a stand of pines just north of Broken Talon Point. She came from a long line of well-bred owls who contributed greatly to the culture of the Northern Kingdoms. She was named for Strix Strumajen, an owl of great courage from the time of the legends.

Struma's parents had high expectations for their daughter from the day she hatched. They tried to provide her with an education befitting her lineage — with lessons in classical literature, music, and etiquette. They hoped she would become a well-rounded and refined young owl and find herself a suitable mate. But Struma

STRIX STRUMA

was a poor student from the start. (Yes, it's true — I could scarcely believe this myself when I heard it.)

"Glaux, was I ever lazy!" Strix Struma told me. "Slept well beyond tween time; some nights, wouldn't even get up until it was First Black. Hardly ever lifted a talon to do anything around the hollow. Thought the sun and moon should rise and set to my liking. You see, Otulissa, I was a smart chick, started counting and reading before my First Meat-on-Bones, if you can believe it. Every grown owl who met me was so impressed. . . . 'Oh, look what little Struma can do! Such an advanced owlet for her age, so gifted!' So by the time I was fully fledged, I thought I had it all figured out. I wouldn't have to do any work, I would just let my 'natural talent' carry me through. Nothing interested me at all, I just wanted to gleek about all night and all day. Some fledgling I was." I still remember her shaking her head and churring abashedly as she related the story.

As Struma got older, her parents' concern for their daughter turned into disappointment. Not only did she seem disinterested in everything, she became downright defiant. She would leave the family's hollow for days at a time, never telling her parents where she had been. Once, she even returned home with her feathers painted like a kraal! Strix Hurth was hags-bent on setting his daughter

43

straight. Having been an instructor in the Academy, he devised a plan.

Deep in the H'rathghar mountains, at the northern edge of Glen Hoole, was a little military camp that the owls of the Kielian League called Little Hoole. Little Hoole was considered a strategically important location in the War of the Ice Claws because it was home to the ruins of an ancient fortress built by the Others called Ghareth's Keep, which, most owls agreed, was impenetrable in the best of conditions. Control of Little Hoole meant control over the vast mountain ranges of H'rathghar. Little Hoole was in a steep, bowl-shaped depression amid the mountains. In fair weather, it was difficult to access, requiring owls to fly over the highest peaks of the mountains. During the winter, when storms incessantly pounded the region, it was all but cut off from the world by swirling winds, snow, and never-lifting fog. With no safe and easy way to leave, owls stationed at Little Hoole would stay there all winter, essentially trapped by weather.

Strix Hurth knew Little Hoole well. The place was run by one of his oldest friends, General Kai, a Snowy from Dark Fowl Island. Strix Hurth himself had been stationed there for a full year as a young owl. It had been the most grueling year of his life. He and his mate thought that was exactly what young Struma needed. At Little Hoole, she would learn discipline and respect for authority. And even though the War of the Ice Claws hadn't officially ended, it seemed that the Kielian League had victory within their grasp. With winter coming, Little Hoole was sure to be one of the safest places in the Northern Kingdoms.

"I nearly screeched my head off! How could they send me to such a glaux-forsaken place?" There was still a hint of outrage in Strix Struma's voice as she continued with her story, but I thought I detected a whiff of nostalgia as well. "But I knew there was nothing I could do to change their minds. Besides, I thought it might be good to get away from my parents, in a way that wouldn't cause them to disown me."

And so, one evening in late autumn, Strix Hurth and Strix Otulinn delivered their delinquent daughter to Glen Hoole. A light snow was falling. It was the most difficult journey that Struma had ever flown. On more than one occasion, she thought that the wildly swirling winds and icy mist would cause her to hurtle into the sheer ice walls of the mountains. And winter hadn't even come yet; this was still the "mild season" in these parts. When she first laid eyes on the icy peaks that she would have to traverse, Struma thought for sure that she would freeze before she reached the glen. She only made it with the guidance of her mum, who, as a weathertrix, was accustomed to this type of flying.

Struma's outlook did not improve at the end of her journey. Little Hoole was as dismal a place as she had imagined. It seemed everything there was a murky shade of gray — including the owls, be they Great Grays, Snowies, or Spotted. She counted fifty or so owls at the camp, and they all moved about in practiced monotony — marching, sharpening ice weapons, moving supplies. Ghareth's Keep itself was a stone monstrosity. Never had Struma seem anything so unwelcoming. But she reckoned that was intentional. This would be where she would sleep every day until spring. She wasn't sure if her gizzard was numb from the prospect or from the cold.

When it came time to light down for the first time in her new home, Struma found that she was exhausted, but could not sleep. And every time she began to doze off, she dreamed of ice walls closing in all around her. When the drill sergeant gave the wake-up call the next evening, Struma marched out of the Keep in a daze, only to find that it wasn't even First Lavender yet.

The night began early for owls at Little Hoole. There was not a single crow in sight in these mountains, so owls were often wakened during the late afternoon to begin their drills. There were marching drills, several types of flying drills, weapon-handling drills, combat drills. . . . so many drills that Struma lost track. Her body ached from First Lavender to First Gray. It was all she could do to climb into her nest at twixt time.

On top of the endless drills, Struma also had to take classes in battle tactics, navigation, geology, and weather interpretation. For the first time in her life, her "natural talents" failed her. At first, she didn't really care that she wasn't doing well in her classes. But soon, it became abundantly clear that failure would not be tolerated. If she didn't master the material covered in class, she was subjected to more drills, less sleep, and scathing looks from the older recruits.

It seemed impossible to make friends at Little Hoole. All the other owls, mostly new recruits, knew of Struma's distinguished lineage and thought of her as little more than a spoiled and self-centered fledgling. Few owls spoke to her unless it was to give her an order. Struma ate alone most nights. Almost a full moon cycle had passed since her arrival. She grew more depressed with each passing day.

The only owl Struma felt at all close to was her geology instructor, an old Snowy named Sarissa. Sarissa herself was from an ancient line of Snowies from Stormfast Island,

and saw something in young Struma that reminded her of herself. It now seemed that she had lived at Little Hoole for ages, but Sarissa remembered those first miserable days vividly. She gave the Spotted Owl encouragement along with a bit of tough love. "Get over yourself, young'un," she told Struma frankly. "No owl is going to like you just for who your ancestors were, and they're certainly not going to appreciate your thinking that you're smarter than every owl in this place. Put in some effort and you might just learn a thing or two."

Since Snowy Owls often nested on the ground in the tundra, understanding the terrain was of vital importance. Spotted Owls, on the other hand, usually lived in dense coniferous forests and had little practical use for this type of knowledge. Nevertheless, geology became Struma's favorite and best subject. She began to look forward to her geology class every night. She found that her outlook was beginning to change. Soon, Struma began to excel in other subjects as well. She was surprised to find battle tactics fascinating. The daily drills grew easier, too, as Struma got stronger. She found that the other young owls were beginning to treat her with a little more respect. There were even a few that she could call friends. Little Hoole might be grueling, but it wasn't such an awful place after all.

Meanwhile, winter had descended upon the H'rathghar mountains with biting ferocity. Snow fell from the sky but never seemed to reach the ground in the bowl-shaped glen. It swirled and drifted and turned the air opaque. The wind howled like wolves night and day. None of this seemed to bother the owls of Little Hoole, for they had been prepared to live in such conditions. What they had not prepared for was what happened at First Black one night.

As the owls carried on with their drills, they heard a distant rumble. Was it an avalanche? Those were not uncommon in the area, but they never happened in Glen Hoole because the slopes surrounding it were so steep that snow could not accumulate on them. But the rumble grew closer. Then, the earth shook.

All the owls of Little Hoole lifted into the air on instinct. Unable to see through the dense snow, they depended on their acute sense of hearing to avoid becoming completely disoriented. Somewhere, an owl cried out, "The Keep! It's coming down!" Stones crashed. Struma heard the noise and back-winged away from the collapsing structure. But there was another noise, and this one came from just behind her. It began as a soft crackling. Within a second, it grew to a deafening explosion. Struma was thrown forward.

When the rumbling and shaking finally stopped, Little Hoole was completely transformed. Struma knew then that she had just experienced her first earthquake. She had read about this in her geology books, but never expected to live through one. She saw that the west wall of Ghareth's Keep had crumbled. Stones littered the ground. A few owls were examining the damage to the Keep. The rest stared incredulously at something behind Struma. Struma turned to see a stunning sight — the familiar bowl-shaped glen had developed a crack high in the western rock face. There was now a narrow passageway into the glen through the mountains. Little Hoole was no longer impenetrable.

Three nights later, as Struma was helping to clear the rubble, she overheard a troubling conversation. General Kai was speaking with Dag, the scout he had sent out after the earthquake, and a few of the instructors.

"How many?" General Kai asked.

"So many that I didn't have time to count, sir! Looks to be in the hundreds, maybe even a thousand!" The scout's voice was filled with dread. Struma had known the Whiskered Screech to be one of the toughest owls in the camp. It was his alarmed tone that caught her attention.

"How could they have found out so fast? They must

have already been amassing their forces when the quake occurred."

"We can still hole up here, in the eastern portion of Ghareth's Keep. They'll never be able to breach it," Maia, the Great Gray who taught weather interpretation, suggested.

General Kai shook his head. "With no protection from the mountains, the Ice Talons can bring in fresh troops whenever they need them. They can besiege us for many moon cycles if we hole up."

Struma's gizzard shuddered. The Ice Talons! She had been sent here to learn discipline, not to be a soldier. Was there going to be a battle? A *real* battle? She continued to listen.

"He's right," Sarissa spoke for the first time. "If we retreat to the Keep, we will die there. We're nearing spring and our supplies are low. Along with our lives, we would lose Little Hoole for sure."

"You're mad if you're suggesting that we engage them. They have us outnumbered ten to one at least!" Maia's voice had begun to sound as frantic as Dag's had.

"We will use the mountains to our advantage. We will meet them in the pass," Sarissa said definitively. Just then, a group of owls flew into the Keep. Struma saw that it was the rest of the instructors and the drill sergeant. She didn't want to be caught eavesdropping, so she left to clear more rubble in another part of the Keep.

Later that night, General Kai called all the owls of Little Hoole together to tell them of the oncoming invasion. The Ice Talons were coming to take Little Hoole and Ghareth's Keep from the Kielian League, and the fifty-some owls here would have to defend it. The enemy was strong, and the owls of the Kielian League were vastly outnumbered. But they would fight, and make a last stand if it came to that. The battle would likely commence tomorrow. Scouts had been posted in the pass to warn them when the enemy was within range. Some of the old-timers took the news with sage stoicism, while the new recruits were clearly shaken. Kai appointed commanders who would explain the tactics and lead sections of troops into battle. Struma listened nervously to the words of the general. She looked over to Sarissa in time to see the Snowy give her a reassuring glance.

After the announcement, General Kai sought Struma out from the crowd. She had been trying to summon her courage, and hoped that the general would help boost her morale. Instead, he said something that, to her surprise, disappointed her greatly. "I promised your father that I would keep you safe, Struma. You are to remain in the east chamber of the Keep. Stay there until I come for you. That's an order." General Kai had fully expected the young Spotted Owl to be relieved.

"No," Struma said squarely. She hadn't thought about what she would say, and she wasn't sure why she said what she said. But it was the answer that her gizzard gave her, and she surprised herself with the composure in her own voice. "I want to fight."

"You're no soldier, young'un."

"Then that means I don't have to take your orders." The defiance of Struma's fledgling days returned. She had never been more sure about anything than she was about the coming battle. "With all due respect, sir, this wretched place has turned me into a better owl, and I have learned to love it and the owls around me. I am no longer a fledgling, and I want to do this." For the first time, Struma felt like a full-grown owl.

General Kai continued to argue with her, but Struma's mind was set. Finally, the Snowy gave in, because he had much more to do before the battle. He assigned Struma to the reserves.

They called it "Operation Breakspear." General Kai and the others had devised a bold strategy. Since the crack was narrow, roughly ten pytes at its widest point, only a few enemy owls would be able to fit through it at once.

The owls of Little Hoole would block the only entrance to the glen by attacking, in waves, in a tight formation inside the passageway. There would be little room to maneuver, and falling back would not be an option. The advantage lay in the terrain. If the Ice Talons were to get through the narrow pass, they would be able to surround the owls of the Kielian League and defeat them easily. By keeping the battle in the pass, General Kai and Sarissa hoped that they could render the enemy's superior numbers useless. All the owls had gone through countless close combat drills, and their skills would be tested now. Three owls had been dispatched to request reinforcements from the Firth of Fangs. Their job would be the most difficult, for they would have to evade the enemy.

"Hoooo-hoo-hoo-hoo-hoo," the first scout barked his warning as he spotted the enemy in the distance. "Hoo-wah," a second scout confirmed.

Fear filled Struma's hollow bones like ice water. Along with the rest of her unit, she was in position along a ledge high up in the narrow passageway. It was First Black. A light snow was falling. It reminded Struma of her journey to Little Hoole. She had flown within pytes of sheer rock faces then, too. To think, she had thought *that* was difficult. As she waited, she heard a disturbance in the glen — a disturbance caused by the beating of a thousand wings.

They were coming. Struma's eyes searched the narrow sliver of sky. First, there was a faint shadow against the moonlight. Within a few heartbeats, the shadow grew closer. They were here.

Seeing the enemy brought about an odd feeling of calm in Struma. The waiting was the hard part. Now, as the battle was about to start, her gizzard unwound. She flexed her talons, unlocking her battle claws. An ice sword lay at her side. She was ready.

"Hold your positions! Hold . . . hold . . ." General Kai commanded. "Assume attack formation, NOW!"

The first unit flew into position. They formed a phalanx — moving as one in close formation. Immediately, the enemy was upon them. A pair of Boreal Owls rushed the phalanx with ice swords in their talons. Struma watched one and then another fall out of the sky as members of the phalanx slashed and stabbed in unison. The sight was surreal. Struma realized that she had never seen death until today. Yet it did not frighten her. Waves upon waves of Ice Talons stormed to the front, flying high above the bodies of their fallen comrades, only to die themselves.

The Kielian League's second unit was called in to replace the first, whose members had begun to tire. A second phalanx flew into position swiftly and precisely as the first fell back. It was a carefully choreographed war dance. This unit was led by Maia. For all her talk of retreating the day before, she fought as fiercely as any owl. She wielded a fearsome ice scimitar and felled a dozen enemies with just a few slashes. Struma saw that at least a hundred Ice Talons had been either killed or wounded, but more kept coming. The losses on the Kielian League's side, meanwhile, were few.

The third unit, led by Sarissa, now replaced the second as smoothly as the second had replaced the first. But, unbeknownst to the fresh crop of fighters, the enemy was about to alter its tactics. Realizing that they were losing despite their numbers, the commanders of the Ice Talons called a stop to the waves and waves of indiscriminate attacks. Instead, the soldiers were to focus on one point in the Kielian League's phalanx, to try to weaken it and break the formation. The enemies swarmed one owl at the top of the passageway, overwhelming him.

To General Kai's horror, the Ice Talons' change in tactics was working. The battle was turning. He was losing soldiers left and right. "Reserves, engage!" he shouted amid the clang of battle claws and ice weapons.

Struma lifted off her ledge with her ice sword in her talons. She flew to a spot in the phalanx that looked thin. Immediately, she was engaged in talon-to-talon fighting.

The enemy was so close that she could scarcely swing her sword. No matter, she had her battle claws. She cut down her first enemy with calculated precision. Her gizzard was on fire. Her muscles and hollow bones, strong and finely honed from the endless drills she endured, took over. It seemed that with the addition of the reserves, the owls of Little Hoole were turning the battle to their favor once again. Another hundred Ice Talons fell, but still more kept coming.

The sun was just beginning to fill the sky with its first orange rays. Struma saw that all three units, as well as other reserve fighters like herself, were now in the pass. They were doing all they could to maintain formation, but they were losing their numbers and confusion was beginning to set in. Meanwhile, she was doing her best to fend off the attackers closest to her. Snow continued to fall, turning the battlefield white. A Barred Owl flew directly at her with battle claws extended. She brought her ice sword up just in time to keep the metal-covered talons from slashing her face. With another thrust of her ice sword, she sent the Barred Owl reeling with a gash in his chest. Within a single heartbeat, a Pygmy Owl took the place of the fallen Barred Owl, her ice splinter coming within striking distance of Struma's eyes. Struma stumbled backward in fright, barely evading the jab. Before she could recover, an enormous Great Gray was upon her, his ice scimitar glistening with blood. In her struggle to regain her balance, her ice sword fell from her talons. In that instant, the world slowed down. *This is it,* Struma thought, *I'm about to die.* Her life did not flash before her eyes, and she felt no fear. She simply watched the blade of her enemy's scimitar come toward her. *Any second now, the world will turn black.* She was sure that the Great Gray was attacking with great haste, but to her, it all seemed so slow, so unreal. *Is this what dying feels like?*

Before she could refocus her eyes, a white blur appeared before her. Sarissa! The Snowy lunged at the Great Gray. The Great Gray flapped his enormous wings once and lunged back. Sarissa expertly parried the Great Gray's attacks, darting back and forth. Finally, she thrust her sword forcefully at the Gray's port wing, almost severing it. *She's done it, she saved my life!* Struma was stunned. But she quickly managed to regain her balance, and picked up her ice sword. She was ready to rejoin Sarissa in battle.

Just then, the dying Great Gray thrashed about wildly, as if in shock. Suddenly, a gash appeared on Sarissa's side, staining her white feathers red. The Gray had slashed her with his scimitar. It would be his last act.

"No!" screamed Struma as she watched her mentor fall from the sky. She dove toward Sarissa in desperation.

"Defend yourself, Struma!" Sarissa yelled as she fell.

Struma turned her head toward the sky just in time to see the Northern Saw-whet who was diving toward her brandishing a deadly ice splinter. *She saved me again*, Struma thought as she came out of her dive with her sword poised to strike.

Struma realized now that Sarissa could not be saved. She needed to focus on the battle, to live to fight another day as the old saying went. She would mourn after the battle was over, but now, she would avenge Sarissa by killing their enemies. Down went the Northern Saw-whet.

On and on the battle went. The situation was growing more dire by the minute for the Kielian League. If the remaining owls of the Kielian League were pushed out of the pass, it would all be over. Struma was more tired than she had *ever* been. Still, she fought on. She looked at her comrades fighting beside her. Their numbers had grown thin while the enemy seemed endless. This was their last stand.

The enemy continued pushing toward the glen. Soon, if she did not die, she would be pushed back into Little Hoole.

Then, without warning, the Ice Talons far back in the pass turned their backs on the glen.

"Incoming!" an owl yelled in the distance. "Friendlies!"

The snow stopped falling and the air was clear for the first time in a moon cycle. "Reinforcements from the Firth of Fangs, sir!" It was Dag calling out to General Kai. Somehow, he had gotten past the Ice Talons at the start of the battle and brought back at least five units of fighting owls from the Firth.

It was utter chaos. The Ice Talons' generals had lost all control over their soldiers. Some tried to surrender while others slashed madly at any owls who went near them. Struma wasn't sure what to do. She was awaiting orders when a Barn Owl came at her, screeching deliriously. He had his ice sword raised within inches of Struma's outstretched wing. Just then, another white blur appeared in front of Struma. *Sarissa?* The ice sword in the Snowy's talons cut down the Barn Owl swiftly and mercilessly.

Was I just saved by a scroom? "Sarissa?" Struma asked disbelievingly.

The Snowy Owl turned to face her. "No. The name is Barran. Glad to be of service." And quickly as she came, Barran left to check on conditions in another part of the battlefield.

The battle was finally over.

The mood at Little Hoole was one of elation. Fifty owls had stood against hundreds and successfully defended what was theirs. Struma was jubilant and heartbroken at the same time. She had survived her first battle, having done her part to defend Little Hoole. But she had also lost a mentor and many friends. After the victory celebration was over, Struma retired to her nest and slept. She slept from Deep Gray to First Lavender, and to Deep Gray the next day. No one could begrudge her sleeping in this time.

Shortly after the battle, Strix Hurth and Strix Otulinn were reunited with their daughter. Struma was going home. As the family was saying their good-byes to General Kai, he whispered to its youngest member, "Well done, Strix Struma." With those words, General Kai bestowed a great honor upon the young Spotted Owl. Since ancient times, Spotted Owls have eschewed honorifics. To distinguish those who show great courage on the battlefield, they are given the title of Strix. Strix Hurth and Strix Otulinn nodded their approval and felt nothing but pride for their daughter.

The Battle of Little Hoole would go down in history as one of the most heroic ever fought. But Strix Struma never boasted about her role in it. She simply called it a "learning experience." She died on the night that she told me this story. I find it fitting that she was as valiant in her first battle as she was in her last. The great tree will forever miss her.

IFGHAR AND LYZE OF KIEL

The following pages came from a diary. I found them in the hidden chamber in Ezylryb's hollow after his death. The diary appears to have been written by Ezylryb's brother, Ifghar. I have taken the liberty of translating it from the original Krakish. The pages were creased and worn, but it was obvious that great care had been taken to preserve them.

There was so much that I didn't know about the strife between these warrior brothers, so much I failed to understand about the lesser brother; so much more to this turnfeather than I ever could have guessed.

From the day I hatched, Lyze took it upon himself to watch out for me. He was in my very first memories, even more so than Ma was. He guided me through every little thing that an owlet does, my First Insect, my First Meat, the first time I branched. . . . I cannot remember a single event in my young life that did not include Lyze. My big brother was always by my side, watching out for me.

He wanted to make me the best owl I could be. He wanted me shrewd — a quality that he thought Lysa had lacked. He wanted me strong — as all warriors of the North were. He wanted me tough — as tough as he

❧ IFGHAR ❧

believed himself to be, and as tough as Pa was when he was alive.

He hadn't watched out for Lysa. He was an owlet himself, after all, and nobody could blame young Lyze. That is, except for Lyze himself.

I don't know exactly what had happened in the year before I was hatched. From what I was able to piece together, Lysa was days from branching when it happened. It was early evening. She was sleeping peacefully in her nest. Ma was out hunting. Pa was on the front lines, as he had been for many nights. And Lyze had just begun branching. He did this on his own, Pa was not there to help him. Too often fathers, and sometimes mothers, were not around to raise their chicks; the war took them away from their homes.

Lyze had hopped through the branches of the tall, slender pine that had been our home. He was almost fully fledged, and so close to flying. From branch to branch he went, getting farther and farther from our hollow. He heard a soft chirp, and looked down to see little Lysa, having woken from her nap, at the edge of our hollow. She looked up at her big brother, longing to join him in his fun. Before Lyze could react, Lysa tumbled down to the ground. Lyze called out in the staccato bark of alarm that we Whiskered Screech Owls use in times of danger.

But it was useless. He watched as a coyote snatched his downy little sister in his jaws, and disappeared into the eventide.

Ma and Pa never talked about it after I was hatched. But I knew it never left their minds. "Be a good big brother, Lyze. Watch out for Ifghar." We both knew what they meant. *Watch out for Ifghar so what happened to Lysa doesn't happen to him.*

My brother loved me, I knew. When Ma, and later on, Lyze, brought back meat from a hunt, he would always insist that I get my fill. When food was scarce, and that was often during this war, I ate like a king. Lyze often insisted that he wasn't hungry or could not eat another bite. Only now do I realize that he had gone hungry on many a night. When I began to walk, Lyze was never more than a few wing beats away, always ready to catch me if I stumbled. "That's it, Chickpea, there you go," he'd say as he steadied me with his wing tips.

The last time I saw Pa was at my First Fur ceremony. He had brought back a snow mouse. The next day, he was killed in combat, stabbed through the heart with an ice sword. "Murdered by those damnable oppressors from the League of Ice Talons," Lyze later told me. Ma fell into a state of despondency.

After that, my brother became my keeper. He was my

father, my mother, my teacher, my confidant, and my commander.

He was hard on me at times, but I knew it was for my own good. Everything he did, he did to make me stronger, savvier, more resilient. When I began branching, he was there to make sure I mastered the perfect technique. "Sharper on the downstrokes, sharper! Listen to your wing beats, you should hear nothing. By Glaux, a squirrel fifty pytes away could hear you coming. Sharper! Quicker!" I remember all of it. When I began flying, and then hunting, there was more of the same. "You can do better than that; if that vole wasn't so slow-witted, it would have gotten away from you for sure. Ready those talons faster next time."

Every once in a while, I got a "Well done, Chickpea," along with an approving nod. Those came rarely, and I yearned for them.

When Lyze came of age, he joined the Kielian League, as all able-bodied owls had done in the Bay of Kiel for nearly two hundred years. He had been looking forward to this since the day that Pa had died. He had long talked of his desires to "avenge his forefathers." As he began his career at the Kielian Military Academy, he became more strict than ever. He was the top cadet in his class. When he was home from training, he would teach me all the new skills that he had learned. Long before most young owls see their first ice sword, I was sparring with one under his stringent tutelage. He had inherited Pa's old battle claws and practiced with them constantly. He even let me fly with them once, "to get the feel," as he said.

What fascinated me most out of everything that Lyze introduced me to were the books he sometimes brought home — his field manuals and battle tactics handbooks. I fell in love with the written word. Soon, I was reading everything I could get my talons on, and pulling out feathers for quills faster than I could grow them. Lyze thought this was "impractical." So I did most of my reading and writing while he was away.

One day, Lyze came back to the hollow that we shared carrying a pair of battle claws in his beak. I could tell they weren't Pa's battered old pair. No, these were breathtaking.

Battle claws

"I had them made special by Orf, the famed blacksmith on Dark Fowl Island," he told me as he slipped his right foot into one. "I had to trade quite a few black rocks and animal skins for them. Called in a personal favor, too." He tilted them back and forth in the morning sunlight. "Orf is thinking of retiring, you know. These might be the last pair of battle claws he ever makes."

They were the most beautiful things I had ever seen. The metal was polished to a gleaming luster. An intricate scroll pattern that resembled cresting waves had been inscribed on the two outermost claws. Each claw tapered to a perfect, deadly point.

"They're magnificent, " I told him.

"They sure are, Chickpea, they sure are. . . ." He slipped his left foot slowly into the other.

Blinding jealousy tore through my gizzard. I lusted after those claws. They were more art than they were weapons. I couldn't tell you exactly why, but they captivated me down to my pin feathers. It would not be the last time that I felt such jealousy over something beautiful that belonged to Lyze.

Lyze watched me as I admired the battle claws with huge, unblinking eyes. Then, a little churr escaped from his beak as he slipped his talons out of the claws. "I had them made for *you*, little brother."

I tilted my head back and forth to make sure my ear slits had not deceived me.

"That's right, Ifghar, they're for you." He held them up for me to see. "But not yet." He pulled them away from my reaching talons. "They'll be yours when you're ready for them. You'll have to grow into them, in body and in spirit."

I couldn't believe it. "Th-thank you, Lyze" was all I managed to say. Of all the things my brother had done for me . . . tears welled in my eyes.

"I don't want gratitude," he told me kindly, "What I want from you is courage and purpose. Show that you're ready to be a warrior of Kiel, and these will be yours."

I nodded and took his words to heart.

Within the year, I enrolled in the Academy. With the skills that Lyze had taught me, I had a head start, and did well. Lyze graduated at the top of his class and went on to join the Glauxspeed Artillery Division. There, he helped to develop a new and devastating fighting technique, one in which owls flew with Kielian snakes on their backs — two attackers moving as one, the Kielian Method, it was called.

That is how I met Gragg of Slonk. He was assigned to me by my commander at the Academy. The Kielian

Method was an instant success. The academy began teaching it to the cadets right away. Gragg was unpopular among his Kielian snake peers, but he was a good fighter. And when he had a bit of bingle juice in him, he became the life of the party. We became fast friends. Having another species on your back for much of the day will do that.

I also met Lil at the Academy. I was reading a book on the history of the Northern Kingdoms when she appeared in the study hollow. She was the most beautiful Whiskered Screech I had ever set eyes upon. She had bright yellow eyes — brighter than the petals of the wildflowers that bloomed on the hills in spring. Short streaks of deep mahogany and snowy white ran through her brown feathers. I imagined myself preening them.

"I think the predecessors to the current regime were on the right track. It'll take strong leadership to unite all these clans. But the Ice Talons are only winning battles, not the minds and hearts of the owls they want to rule."

Her voice was melodic and confident. I was so surprised that she was speaking to me, that I barely understood her words.

"Uh, pardon?" I said idiotically.

"The chapter you're reading" — she pointed at my book with her talon — "on the regime under General Geirleif."

"You're familiar with General Geirleif?" I was pleasantly surprised. Not many of my classmates read history books these days, most were preoccupied with manuals on weaponry and attack strategies.

"I try to understand some of the basic concepts," she replied modestly.

That's how our nightly discussions began. I had found a kindred spirit in Lil. She was as intelligent as she was beautiful. After our nightly drills and before the sun rose, we would meet in the study hollow and talk. We talked about subjects that other owls, Lyze included, had dismissed as academic frivolity. She opened my mind to so many things, and I like to think that I did the same for her.

I loved her, of course, but I was a complete mooncalf when it came to courtship. I had no idea where to begin. The very idea of it filled me with a sense of panic a hundred times worse than did any battle. Our relationship remained one of scholarly admiration.

Soon, Lil and I both graduated. Lyze was promoted to Commander, the youngest ever in the history of the Kielian League. I was assigned to Glauxspeed Artillery Division, just as Lil was, and Lyze had been. But I was in a different unit, stationed far to the south, and rarely saw either of them. I thought of them both often.

Because we flew so well together, Gragg and I remained

a team. We were thrown into battles immediately. I counted many moments when I thought for sure that my life was about to end. But somehow, Gragg and I always made it through. He was a great tactician, it turned out. In times of danger, he always made the right choice. "On my mark, increase drag, she'll fly right by us!" he said once as we were being pursued by two armored Snowies. I never would have pulled a move like that without Gragg. I owe my life to his quick thinking.

It was rare for Lyze and me to have the same night off. When we did, we would perch high in a tree and catch up on what was going on in our lives. At the end of those nights, he became my caring big brother again and I his "Chickpea."

On one such occasion, after a lovely late night flight, he told me that he had met a female. *The* female.

"She's fierce, this one! Beautiful, too. Can't wait for you to meet her." He beamed with joy. "We went on our first courtship flight a few nights ago. I think I might ask her to be my mate soon."

I couldn't remember ever seeing him this happy. And I was thrilled for him.

"How 'bout you, Chickpea?"

I hadn't told him about Lil. What was there to tell?

That I was woefully inadequate when it came to the court-
ing ritual? That I turned into a gibbering puffin at the very
thought? Of course I didn't want to sound like an imma-
ture little owlet to my brother, he would expect me to be
plucky and bold. "I don't know.... There might be this
one owl that I have my eyes on, but ... I don't know. I'm
not sure...."

I think I must have wilfed out of self-consciousness.
Lyze sensed my discomfort. "Well, you're young, you'll
have plenty of time to worry about finding a mate."

Just then, two of Lyze's buddies from his unit landed
on a neighboring branch, a Great Gray named Loki and a
Northern Saw-whet named Blix. They made quite a pair —
Blix's entire body was smaller than half of Loki's facial disk.

"Ahoy! You must be Ifghar."

"And you must be Blix. Your prowess with ice splin-
ters is well-known, even on my side of the bay." I spoke
the truth. I had heard some amazing tales about the little
owl. He had suffered a wound in the Battle of Firthvir,
and was given commendations for bravery.

"Oh, no, that's nothing. My main job in the field these
days is to inspect the ice weapons and battle claws to make
sure they're up to snuff."

I liked this humble owl.

"Whooo-ooo-ooo," said the Great Gray, "and what has your brother told you about me? Chicklet? Chickbean? What is it that Lyze here calls you?" Loki churred.

"My name is Ifghar," I said crossly. "And he has only told me that his friend Loki was a big Great Gray." I wish Lyze hadn't told them about the Chickpea thing. It was fine between the two of us, endearing even. But who would respect me as a commander with a nickname like Chickpea?

"Give it a blow. I was just being friendly, Chickling."

I didn't like this owl.

"Watch it, Loki. Don't tease my brother." Lyze turned to me. "Pay no attention to him, Ifghar, he's just a joker."

"So, you tell him about your courtship flight yet?" Blix asked Lyze.

Lyze nodded, and turned back to me. "Seems like the whole division is finding mates these days. Loki here is waiting for two eggs to hatch!"

Some owl actually mated with this nincompoop? She must be yoiks. But all I said was, "Congratulations."

"Ifghar here is in a bit of a gollymope, trouble approaching a female," Lyze said to his buddies, feigning a whisper. *Racdrops!* I wish he hadn't told them that either.

"I didn't say that! It's nothing, I . . . There is no female. . . ." I began to stammer.

But it was too late, Loki and Blix gave me a merciless ribbing for the next half hour. "Oh, boo-hoo-hoo, poor little Chickbean, so lonesome, can't find a mate. . . ." Loki whined in his best owl-chick voice, all the while making exaggerated preening motions and yarping a pellet at the same time. Blix churred so hard that he fell off his perch twice. Lyze seemed to have found it quite amusing, too.

When the laughter finally died down, Loki hopped over to the branch that I was perched on. "Listen, Ifghar." *He called me by my name!* He lowered his voice to a serious tone, "All joking aside, let me make it up to you for all this fun we've been having at your expense. I will tell you a sure way to win over your female."

This was the first time that this owl had spoken to me like I was an equal, instead of some owlipoppen-cuddling chick. I was still suspicious, but curious about what he would say. "Go on."

"In the olden days, before the war began, all male Megascops — that means all Screech Owls, like you — had to prove their worthiness to females before they were accepted as mates."

I was intrigued.

Loki continued, "Now, pay attention, this was a very important ritual." His voice was now at a whisper, as if he were telling me some great secret. "They proved their worthiness by plucking out all their whiskers."

"All their whiskers? That's outrageous!"

"It's true, all the noble owls did this, owls from the best families. If you pluck out all your whiskers, you'll win your female for sure. Isn't that right, Blix?"

"You know more about that stuff of yore than I do," Blix said, shaking his head.

Lyze said nothing.

That made sense, I supposed. I thought back to some of the books that I had read on other species of birds. There was one species whose males would puff out these great big bubbles on their chests to attract females. Another would make their tail feathers stand straight up in the air. I supposed plucking one's whiskers wasn't so far-fetched. Lil was a cultured owl and a descendant of one of the oldest lines of Whiskered Screeches in the Northern Kingdoms. Perhaps she *would* be moved by such a gesture.

The night ended with more "male bonding" as Lyze called it. Despite all the teasing, it was a nice respite from the training and fighting. Just before Loki flew off, he lifted a foot toward his face, and with a wink he whispered, "Don't forget about the whiskers."

I would not forget about the whiskers. I knew that I had an opportunity to see Lil during my next leave. That's when I would do it.

I knew it would smart. I thought I would be prepared having pulled out all those feathers for quills in the past. Apparently, I was not so prepared. It *hurt*! My eyes teared up with every yank. It wasn't a simple task, either — I had to borrow a pair of tongs from the blacksmith to get at my whiskers. Afterward, I looked at my reflection in a puddle. With the bald patch around my beak, I looked ridiculous. Nevertheless, I was pleased with myself. *If this is what it takes, then so be it.* I planned to surprise Lil with my "cosmetic improvements" the following night. What I didn't realize was that it would be one of the worst nights of my life.

"BWA-HA-HA-HA-HA! Wha? Why? Ah-ha-ha-ha-ha! Oh, dear . . . Ha-ha-ha-ha!" Lil could not stop laughing long enough to catch her breath. "Oh, dear! Ifghar! That's . . . Ah-ha-ha-ha-ha-ha!"

It was clear that she did not interpret my gesture as it was intended. What was I to say? *I did this to impress you?* I stood there, stunned. Then, it dawned on me. *Pay no attention to him, Ifghar, he's just a joker.* Wasn't that what Lyze had said? *What a fool I was! I'm going to kill that frinking Great Gray.*

To make matters worse, I saw my brother circle above me and Lil, coming in for a landing.

"What's so . . . ?" Lyze stopped mid-sentence as he saw my face. "Oh, Ifghar. You didn't!"

I was humiliated. I could not meet my brother's gaze. How I wished for the tree we perched on to be swallowed by the earth right then. "I . . . I thought . . ."

"Wait, is this because of what Loki said? You took Loki *seriously*? He's the biggest trickster in the division! I told you that! He was just hazing you!"

At that moment, I hoped against all hope that Lyze would not tell Lil of how easily I had been bamboozled. My gizzard was convulsing. I was still trying to think of a plausible explanation that I could give to Lil when Lyze said the words that I had least expected to hear.

"So, I see you've met Lil, my soon-to-be mate." He hugged her close to him.

A thousand ice daggers pierced my heart. *His* soon-to-be mate? Had I been in the air I would have certainly gone yeep. Almost immediately, I could feel my gizzard fill up with rage. I was angry at Lyze for not telling me the truth behind Loki's "advice." I was angry at him for stealing Lil from me. I was angry at him for utterly failing to watch out for his little brother. But I was most angry at myself for being such a mooncalf.

Lil had finally stopped laughing now. "Oh, Lyze, Ifghar and I have known each other for ages, ever since the Academy. I just didn't know he was your brother. Well, I guess we'll be family soon, Ifghar!"

She looked so happy, so radiant. That only devastated me more.

I can't remember what happened after that. It was as if time stopped and the world became a blur.

For the next several weeks, I threw myself into combat. Evidently, losing all my whiskers as well as all my dignity did not affect my abilities to fight. I let go of all fear. At the Tridents, with Gragg on my back, I took down a dozen enemy owls within a quarter of an hour. I slashed at them with my ice sword left and right, unleashing my rage. Gragg, emboldened by my ferocity, struck swiftly and lethally. We were unstoppable. I was anesthetized by the carnage that, at one time, would have sickened me. Mere days later, the two of us scattered an entire squadron of Ice Talon infantry owls at Firthmore. Only after the battle was over did I realize that an ice splinter had grazed my breast. For that, I received the Blue Heart of Valor, an honor given to owls of the Kielian League who are wounded by the enemy in battle. On the night that I received my award, I was also promoted to Commander.

Lyze appeared at the award ceremony. In his beak, he held the battle claws made by the famed blacksmith Orf on Dark Fowl Island. He had kept them polished and gleaming, just as they had been when I first laid my eyes on them. I had almost forgotten about those battle claws. But seeing them again reminded me how badly I had wanted them all those years ago.

"Tonight, they go to their true owner." Lyze laid the battle claws at my feet. "I'm proud of you, Ifghar."

"Thank you, Lyze." I managed to say as I tried to hold back tears.

How could I have been angry with him? How petty of me. He had watched out for me the best he could, yet I blamed him for my despair. No more. Tonight, I would vow to be happy for my brother, happy for him, and for Lil.

"Where's Lil?" I asked casually, hoping that my emotions would not betray me.

"She's home, resting. She has just laid an egg."

An egg! "That's fantastic news!" I wrapped my wing around Lyze. And indeed, I was happy for them.

I was put on medical leave to allow my wound to heal. My new battle claws hung on a peg in my hollow, unused. My injury was a bit more serious than I had originally thought. I was barely able to fly, so I spent most of my waking hours reading and writing. I had forgotten how much I enjoyed that.

The selection of books available to me at the base was limited. I asked Gragg to go to the Academy and bring me some fresh reading material. He brought back a lackluster selection, including a manual on battlefield recovery, a book on troop movement, and one on hunting in the desert. All boring stuff meant for cadets. Then, one book caught my attention: *A Treatise on Unification and the Foundation for Peace in the Northern Kingdoms*, by Bylyric. General Bylyric? Leader of the Ice Talons? The brutal tyrant and our most hated enemy? Writing about peace, of all things.

I began reading.

Some one hundred and seventy years ago, the Ice Talons sought to strengthen our region by unifying all the kingdoms of the Everwinter Sea. It was thought to be the start of a vigorous campaign to unify and centralize all the Northern Kingdoms. They were met with resistance by a few of its neighboring clans. The neighboring clans, including those on Stormfast Island and elsewhere in the Kiel Bay, began a resistance movement. The resistance was rooted in a desire to remain independent mainly in the area of trade.

I had always been taught that the Ice Talons had started the war out of their desire to conquer. This was the first I had heard of an attempt at unification. I kept reading.

> *The path to peace and prosperity has often been obscured by misinformation. What began as an earnest concern on the part of the resistance has become a faulty ideology. To achieve peace, this ideology must be defeated. A victory for the Ice Talons would lead to the stability and peace that the region desperately needs.*

The more I read, the more it all made sense. How many generations of owls have lived and died in the war? I thought of Lyze and Lil, and of their egg. I thought of Pa, whom I barely knew before war took him from us. I thought of Lysa, whom I never knew. I thought of the scores of owls I had killed and watched be killed. What was I really fighting for? I only fought because that was what owls did in the Bay of Kiel. It was as if a dense fog had suddenly cleared to reveal a sky full of stars. All these years, the Kielian League has sought victory while it should have sought peace.

Lyze. I had to tell Lyze, he would understand.

"Have you gone completely yoiks?" From the moment I told him of my plan, Lyze was outraged. "Bylyric is a tyrant and an oppressor!"

Again and again I tried to make him see my point. "I know Bylyric has been ruthless in the past. But have you ever considered that he may be far-seeing as well? If we could only speak with him, off the battlefield. . . ." My arguments had won over Gragg just the day before, but they were utterly ineffective at convincing Lyze.

"No!" he barked. "What you're suggesting is treasonous!"

I was shocked and dismayed. How could my brother not see my logic, not even in the slightest? He was a reasonable owl, a bright owl. But at that moment, his pride and the strength of tradition overpowered all reason.

"Please, Lyze. If we could only get our side to consider surrender. Then, we could live in peace for the first time in almost two hundred years," I implored.

"No! These tyrants have done us wrong, made life in the Bay of Kiel miserable for generations of owls. I will not surrender, and neither will any of my fellow warriors. They want to crush us, Ifghar! And I mean to obliterate them!"

"Perhaps they want peace, too."

Lyze shook his head in disbelief. He turned to look at my battle claws. "I was wrong. You are not ready." He removed them from their place above my nest in my hollow. "Not only are you not ready, you are not *worthy* of these. You have shamed yourself to our forefathers in glaumora."

With my battle claws in his beak, he flew out of my hollow.

I began to pursue him. I wasn't sure what I would do if I caught up to him. Would I fight him to reclaim my battle claws? Plead with him some more? Apologize and tell him that I was wrong? In the end, I never found out. My injury was still not completely healed, and I could not fly very quickly or very far. I lost him when I was forced to land in a fir tree, no longer able to continue.

I fear that I have caused a rift between me and my brother that will be impossible to mend. I also fear that I am a part of a war that will never end. I do not take what I am about to do lightly. I know the consequences will likely be dire.

Tomorrow, I will go to General Bylyric, alone. The next day, perhaps all of the Northern Kingdoms will have peace.

Perhaps, for once, I will be the one watching out for my big brother.

THE PLONK SINGERS AND HONEYVOX

For as long as there have been owls at the Great Ga'Hoole Tree, a singer from the renowned Plonk family has tolled the passage of daily life there. The Snow Rose was the very first of these singers. Once a gadfeather, she accepted Hoole's offer to become the great tree's resident singer, thus starting a tradition that has lasted a thousand years. Plonk, of course, was not the family name that the Snow Rose was born into. She chose to take the name as a way of marking the new chapter in her life. Plonk was derived from the Krakish word *plonkvir*, which means "enjoyment" and "delight."

The Plonk family of Snowy Owls, all descendants of the Snow Rose, have since flourished in the Northern and Southern kingdoms. They have sent singers to every community in every kingdom for generations. The most refined and most talented singer in each generation has always been chosen to reside at the great tree. Every one of these singers has been a fixture at the tree, and has

✿ HONEYVOX ✿

brought much joy to the owls who have lived there. When an owl from another kingdom speaks of the splendid culture of Ga'Hoole, the Plonk singer is inevitably mentioned.

Currently, the resident singer is Madame Brunwella Plonk. Of course, no one at the tree ever refers to her as "Brunwella," she is simply "Madame Plonk." I am not sure how that tradition started but it seems that all singers have been referred to only as "Madame Plonk" or "Sir Plonk" in person. I can only deduce that it was done as a sign of reverence. In the annals, their full names are used, but only to distinguish them from one another. I will do the same here.

Madame Brunwella and I are as different as owls can be. She can be a bit, oh, how should I put it, ostentatious at times. What with her "apartments" and "whirlyglass"

Whirlyglass

and other doodads . . . why, I cannot help find some of those things appallingly vulgar. But, at the great tree, we are free to live as we wish. And it's her choices that make her the owl she is. I appreciate our differences almost as much as I appreciate her songs. Her voice and her harp have gently lulled me to sleep on many mornings ever since I was a mere owlet. I am glad to have her at the tree, despite her flaws.

Before Madame Brunwella Plonk, scores of Plonk Snowies have graced the tree. And each has enriched the tree in his or her own way.

It was Madame Cornelia Plonk who first brought the great grass harp to the tree. No one is quite sure who built it or where it came from (I plan to make this the topic of one of my research projects in the future), but it was instantly loved by every owl who heard it. The sound it makes is sweet, yet haunting; soft, yet resounding. The instrument is strung with different lengths of various types of grasses. Long, wide blades can be found in the lower octaves, while only the thinnest reeds are used in the highest octave. Today, the harp can be found in the gallery of the Great Hollow, where it can be heard from anywhere in and around the tree.

Marthe, Madame Cornelia's nest-maid snake, quickly became a harp virtuoso. She would weave through the strings so effortlessly that it seemed as if she and the harp shared a soul. She and Madame Cornelia complemented each other perfectly — the sound of the Snowy's voice and the music of the harp melded together to create something much greater than the sum of its parts. Marthe was also the celebrated founder of the harp guild. Not only did she teach other nest-maid snakes to play the harp, she invented a way for multiple snakes to weave through the harp's strings at once so that a beautiful harmony emanated from the instrument, stirring listeners' deepest feelings. Since Marthe's time, hundreds of nest-maid snakes have been a part of the illustrious harp guild, the most artistic and prestigious of the snake guilds. Our own Mrs. Plithiver, Soren's family's nest-maid snake, has continued the tradition. She has been an indispensable member of the guild for many seasons as the G-flat, and has attained the rarefied position of sliptween.

Since the time of Hoole, no owl has challenged the supremacy of the Plonk singers of the great tree — except one.

During an especially cruel winter, a Tropical Screech Owl, a stranger to the Guardians, came to the Great Ga'Hoole Tree to seek shelter from the harsh winds and relentless snow that had battered the land for weeks. The governing owls decided to allow him to stay a short while even though he was not requesting to become a Guardian, for it was the compassionate thing to do.

The stranger was a singer who went by the name of Honeyvox, although he always introduced himself as "the World-renowned Honeyvox."

"Greetings and salutations! I am the World-renowned Honeyvox, but of course, you already knew that," he'd say.

Nobody at the great tree had ever heard of him.

Honeyvox constantly boasted of having sung for all the birds in the land, eagles and whooper swans in the north, and some fantastical purple flamingos in the south. (Ridiculous, of course. We all know that flamingoes are pink).

"The flamingo! Oh, Fernando — dear, dear Fernando. Lovely, lovely bird. Adored my rendition of the 'New Moon Ballad,' he did. Begged me to stay, absolutely begged, I tell you. 'Oh, Honeyvox,' he'd say, 'how are we to live our lives without hearing your bewitching voice every day?' Alas, I had to be quite firm with him, you see. I told him that I simply must go north to share my gift with other birds.

"Ah, and I must tell you about Fiona and Dougal and their darling, darling cygnets. Those little ones . . . always trying to imitate me with their little 'whoop-whoops.' Imitation is the sincerest form of flattery, you know. And then they'd giggle. Oh, I suppose they knew as well as I did that my voice cannot be emulated, and were simply laughing about their own effort. Why, they were always giggling when I was around. Just couldn't get enough of me. I would have sung for them longer had they not flown off. Something about an early migration for the family that year, just upped and disappeared one day. Strange birds, migrators. Oh, but they must have been very sad that I could not go with them, I'm sure."

On and on Honeyvox went. He talked to any owl who would listen to him. Sometimes, he'd talk to no one at all. Honeyvox was also fond of bingle juice. This he made clear, having carried his own supply all through his difficult voyage.

To most owls, especially those who knew anything about music, Plonk was a household name. But Honeyvox claimed that he had never heard of the famous singing family.

"Plonk, you say? No, no, doesn't ring a bell. Snowies, you say? With that 'kroo-kroo kroo-kroo' call, I never would have guessed that they made very good singers. Well, to each his own I suppose."

Sir Lucien Plonk, the well-loved singer of the tree at the time, was clearly offended. But being the dignified owl he was, he held his beak.

The owls of Ga'Hoole listened to Honeyvox sing on many a night during his stay. He was grateful for the Guardians' hospitality and insisted on showing his appreciation with the "gift of song." He also insisted that the harp guild accompany him every time. Sir Lucien magnanimously agreed, even though the harp guild wasn't too happy. He noted that, for such a small owl, Honeyvox did have a booming, though not especially refined, voice.

Honeyvox sang so much and so often, that Sir Plonk was hardly able to get a single note in. The owls of the tree enjoyed Honeyvox's singing for the first few days. It was a change of pace, after all. By the fifth night, however, the owls were clamoring for Sir Lucien Plonk to make his return. Honeyvox was singing the same two songs again and again. "That moon has dwenked already!" some owls would say under their breaths — one could only listen to the "New Moon Ballad" so many times, especially when the moon wasn't even newing.

On the seventh day of Honeyvox's stay, the snowstorm finally let up. The owls of the great tree assumed that their visitor would be on his way as soon as weather permitted. Yet, Honeyvox lingered on. Days turned into weeks. He could always be found in the gallery of the great hollow, trying to get the harp guild to accompany him on one more song. "Play it again, nesties!" he'd say. He was a freeloader, everyone figured. But it was also clear that he had become enamored with the music of the great grass harp.

One night, Honeyvox asked Sir Lucien to "talk shop" over a cup of milkberry tea.

Honeyvox got right to the point, "Say, old Snow, I've come to fancy that harp of yours quite a bit, you see. Would you be disposed to selling it to me? Perhaps we could work out some sort of . . . arrangement. The other owls don't have to know."

The Snowy was taken aback. "Well, I never! You are a presumptuous owl, aren't you? Absolutely not! That harp is a treasure of Ga'Hoole, it shall not leave this tree!"

Great grass harp

"Quite right, quite right," Honeyvox replied, a bit too readily, "I don't know what I was thinking. Foolish idea, obviously. Never mind, sir. Never mind."

His plan having failed, Honeyvox knew he had to find another way. But how? He couldn't imagine ever singing again without the accompaniment of the harp. He realized, too, that even if he was able to get the harp away from the tree, there would be no one to play it — the nest-maid snakes of the harp guild were the only ones who could play the instrument. And it was clear that the stewards of the tree wanted him to leave.

Before Honeyvox knew it, he was coming up on the second month of his stay. He was running out of time. He stayed up all day to think. *Why take the harp with me when I can simply stay with the harp? But, they would never have two resident singers here. Blast it!*

Sir Lucien Plonk was an obstacle. Honeyvox would have to get rid of him somehow. He couldn't kill the Snowy, that would be . . . unseemly. He must find another way. By early evening, he had found the solution. It was one that would require guile and unwavering nerves on the part of the Tropical Screech. He swallowed a good glug of bingle juice for courage, and flew off to the infirmary hollow.

Bloodroot is a plant that's commonly used by the healer owls of Ga'Hoole to this day. Its juice is used to treat a myriad of symptoms from sore throats to gray scale. In small doses, it helps to relieve discomfort. In large doses, it is highly toxic. It was rumored that it could damage a bird's throat, causing it to become permanently mute. Honeyvox hoped that there was truth to this rumor. Just before all the other owls woke, he gathered all the bloodroot juice he could find and stole quietly out of the infirmary.

When night fell, Honeyvox approached Sir Lucien. He would have to choose his words carefully so as not to raise suspicion. He anxiously took another slug of his bingle juice. "Say, Sir Lucien, I hope there are no hard feelings between us. I meant no disrespect the other night. Why don't you have a drink with me in the guest hollow . . . to, um, set things right?"

To Honeyvox's relief, Sir Lucien graciously agreed.

In the guest hollow, where Honeyvox had been staying for the last many weeks, he set out two nut cups. He filled both with his own special reserve of bingle juice. Into one of the cups, he added a stiff dose of the bloodroot juice he had stolen. Luckily for him, bloodroot is odorless, and its slightly sour taste was easily masked by the much stronger flavor of the bingle juice.

It was almost time. Honeyvox started to feel a little wobbly in the gizzard. He wasn't sure if it was the jitters or the bingle juice that was making his head spin.

Sir Lucien arrived exactly when he said he would. The two owls awkwardly exchanged pleasantries. They talked of the weather and of the coming spring. . . . Boring, pointless conversation that Honeyvox could barely pay attention to. All the while, he eyed Sir Lucien's cup nervously — the Snowy had not taken a single sip while his own cup was already empty, despite having been refilled twice.

Down the hatch, you wretched owl! Go on, take a sip. For the love of Glaux, just one sip!

"Oh, the time of the Silver Rain can be so lovely, my favorite time of the year, really," Sir Plonk droned on and on. It was a wonder that the old owl didn't grow thirsty with all this chitchat.

Honeyvox nodded, and then nodded some more while trying to think of a way to get the Snowy to drink his poison. He kept refilling his own cup in an attempt to send a subliminal message to his guest. *Driiiink, Sir Plonk, driiiink. . . .*

Finally, in desperation, he raised his own empty cup. "How about a toast, then? To . . . say . . . music!"

Sir Lucien thought it peculiar that the Tropical Screech would change the subject so abruptly. Why, he was just telling him about the slim vines that cascaded down from the branches of the great tree, and how they were about to turn a pretty shade of silver any day now. But Honeyvox was a strange little owl, and he was happy to bring this awkward little get-together to an end. So he, too, raised his glass. "To music."

The next few seconds felt like days to Honeyvox. First, the Snowy held that cup aloft in his talon for far too long in his toasting gesture. As he lowered it, he swirled the cup deliberately, first clockwise, then counterclockwise. Then, he examined the liquid with his yellow eyes for what seemed like an entire moon cycle.

Does he suspect?

"I've always found bingle juice to have the most lovely color."

Oh, stop looking at it, just drink it! "Of course, lovely color, of course."

Finally, Sir Lucien raised the cup to his beak and took a small sip. As the Snowy swallowed the concoction, Honeyvox's gizzard nearly sprang out of his body.

I've done it! I've actually done it!

But had he?

Having drunk the toast, Sir Lucien excused himself. Something about it being time for "Night Is Done." Honeyvox hardly noticed the other owl's exit. He was overwhelmed by elation, a sense of his own power, and just a touch of guilt. He was practically bouncing from wall to wall in the guest hollow. He needed to settle himself down. Some bingle juice should do the trick. Honeyvox picked up the nut cup next to him and swigged its contents in one gulp.

That morning, Honeyvox lighted down in his nest with a sense of accomplishment. Tomorrow, the owls of the Great Ga'Hoole Tree would find Sir Lucien Plonk mute, never to sing again. Soon, they would need a new singer. And conveniently, he, the world-renowned Honeyvox, would be there.

As Honeyvox went to the dining hollow for tweener the next night, he noticed a commotion. Several of the rybs of the tree, along with numerous other owls, were huddled around the center of the room. As he got closer, he realized that Sir Lucien was at the center of the crowd. This, he expected. But what came next, he did not expect.

Sir Lucien spoke.

"Oh, there you are, Honeyvox. Strangest thing. My voice seems to have grown awfully hoarse after our drink last night. Say, what sort of bingle juice was it?" Sir Lucien rasped. "Oh, I sound downright dreadful."

Honeyvox froze. Perhaps his plan had failed. Perhaps the bloodroot hadn't worked after all. But it was all right; Sir Lucien was in no condition to sing, and no one suspected him of foul play.

98

There was nothing wrong with that bingle juice, old friend. I haven't the faintest idea what could have happened. A nasty cold perhaps?

Honeyvox meant to say those words, but they did not come out of his beak. In fact, no sound came out at all, no matter how hard he tried. He stood with his beak gaping. The events of the previous night flashed before him. And then, the world flipped on its side.

Over the next few nights, the Guardians pieced together what had happened. They discovered what was left of the stolen bloodroot in the guest hollow. Traces of the juice could still be found in the nut cup. Sir Lucien's voice steadily improved. Within a week, he was singing again. He told the other owls of Honeyvox's offer to buy the harp, and his invitation for the two owls to have a drink. It appeared that the small amount of bloodroot ingested by Sir Lucien was not enough to cause permanent damage. He, being a large Snowy Owl, recovered within a few days. Honeyvox, in his jubilation, had inadvertently drunk out of Sir Lucien's cup. Being a much smaller owl, the toxic effects of the bloodroot hit him most brutally. He would never sing or speak again. It was the realization of his most terrible mistake that had caused him to faint in the dining hollow.

Honeyvox was asked to leave the tree. The Guardians

were far from unsympathetic, however. Instead of banishing him to the wild, they escorted him to the Glauxian Brothers' retreat in the Northern Kingdoms. Silence is a way of life there, and Honeyvox would be able to live out the rest of his life in meditation and repentance.

Little more was written about the World-renowned Honeyvox. But the annals note that, as one of his last acts, Sir Lucien Plonk invited a dying Glauxian Brother, a silent Tropical Screech Owl, to hear him sing at the great tree. It is said that this owl died contentedly while listening to the music of the great grass harp.

THEO

Theo, the first blacksmith of the owl world, is known as the "father of metals." His contributions to the development of our culture and our civilization have been monumental. He made the first battle claws, the first tools of the forge, and many things that have since become a part of our lives at the tree. You have heard much of his story, through the words of Grank, the first collier, and from the rest of the legends. But I have discovered many more historical twists and turns in the tale of this humble Great Horned. This additional information

❧ THEO ❧

comes to me from the recent discovery of what are called the "Theo Papers," which were found in the Sixth Kingdom.

As you already know, Theo was a gizzard-resister, an owl who doesn't believe in war or fighting. He believed that there was always a better way to settle disputes. (This is a subject about which I, to this day, have mixed feelings.) However, in a time of hagsfiends and nachtmagen, when the heir to the throne, young Hoole, was in danger, Theo had little choice but to fashion the most devastating weapon that owlkind has ever known. How he hated being in that position. How any of us would hate to be in that position — not knowing if you would achieve the greatest good by following or defying your most gizzardly instincts.

Theo began to think of himself as a facilitator of violence. Other owls of the tree, Hoole and Grank included, believed the blacksmith to be a hero. But it was impossible to convince Theo of this. Battle claws, and the Rogue blacksmiths who made them, were beginning to spring up everywhere in the world of owls. The weapon that once was used to defeat the most treacherous of enemies became commonplace even in minor skirmishes. It seemed that Grank was right, everyone wanted a pair. The deadly weapon had begun to spread as virulently as any disease. There was a plague of battle claws!

Never was Theo more tortured than upon the return of Ivar from a routine mission. A boisterous knight, and a nephew of Lord Rathnik's, Ivar and two other owls were dispatched to help quell a kraal uprising near the Bay of Fangs. Ivar came back to the tree during a full moon, earlier than anyone had expected.

The owl flying wildly toward our tree was not the same strapping young Spotted Owl who had left half a moon cycle before. There was a collective gasp from the tree as the owls saw the bizarre track of his flight. It was Theo who first realized what had happened when he spotted Ivar's starboard foot hanging limply beneath his body. As he angled his wings to land, Ivar began to shout, "Move aside! MOVE! I don't think I can —" With that, he crashed onto a branch, knocking over two perched owls in the process, and slid into the trunk with a thud.

Then, all the owls saw. Ivar's right foot had been severely mutilated. It was covered in dried blood and looked as if it was almost completely severed from his leg. These owls had been hardened by battle, and were no strangers to the sight of blood. Even still, Lord Rathnik gave a lurch and looked away.

"The mission was going well," Ivar spoke between gasps of pain. "We were dispersing the kraals that had settled in the area, and we thought we were nearly finished. In fact, most of the pirates were quite reasonable, agreeing to leave without any threat of violence. Then, their provisional leader, a young hot-talon — I think Sitka was her name — started to inquire about our battle claws, and how she might be able to get her talons into a pair of her own. We told her that it was a rather complex new technology involving fire and rare metals. She then tried to barter for them. Well, there was no way any of us were willing to give up our battle claws." Crude battle claws were being made all over the Northern and Southern kingdoms. But battle claws of this quality — fiendishly sharp and precisely balanced — only came from the forge of Theo. Ivar continued, "Two days later, dozens of them ambushed us while we slept." Ivar's voice began to trail off. "They killed Johan and Lar."

Johan and Lar were the two owls who had accompanied Ivar on this mission. They were battle-seasoned veterans and well-loved by their fellow members of the Ice Regiment of H'rath.

Theo listened in horror, then wilfed. He was a quivering shadow of his former self.

"I only escaped with my life because I was sleeping in

a different hollow. I heard what was happening and flew out. I fought off six or seven of them, but they backed me into an ice notch and I was overcome. They wanted my battle claws. The left set slipped off quite easily, but the right . . . Well, I guess they wanted it badly enough that they didn't care if my foot came off with it. When they got the battle claws, they scattered. I didn't even know which one of them to pursue. Kraal cowards! But I was in no shape for anything by that time except a homebound flight. Luckily, a robust following breeze began to blow. I doubt if I could have made it without it. So, I flew all the way back without stopping. I knew that if I had tried to land, I might not have been able to take off again." Ivar paused, and then babbled incoherently before falling into unconsciousness.

The outlook for Ivar was grim. You see, during the time of the legends, owlkind's understanding of medicine and the healing arts was still in its rudimentary stage. Injuries such as Ivar's almost always meant death. Often, the flesh would fester, and the injured owl would die slowly, in a terrible fevered state. Even if he survived a successful amputation, walking and standing on a perch would be impossible. And as for flying, well, it is true, we owls have wings. But, without feet to connect us back to the earth, we cannot really fly.

Vreta, the healer at the great tree, did all she could for Ivar that night. The sickly sweet smell that she detected could only mean that the flesh was beginning to rot. The mangled right foot could not be saved. Even with the numbing herbs the pain must have been excruciating when Vreta amputated the foot, but Ivar survived.

As the sun rose, Theo sat with the broken knight as he drifted in and out of consciousness. A devastating wave of regret and sorrow swept over the Great Horned Owl. *I am the cause of this. By Glaux, how far I have strayed from my path. . . .* Theo looked at his own talons and thought back to the day when Grank agreed to take him on as an apprentice. He never thought it would lead to this. *I wanted to make good things, useful things. . . .*

Day turned into night, and there was no change in Ivar's condition. That was good news, Theo supposed. Realizing that he could do no more for Ivar, Theo returned to his forge near the roots of the tree. He wanted to be alone, to think about the events that had come to pass. The Glauxian Brothers have always placed great importance on silent meditation. Yes, meditation was what Theo needed more than anything else at the moment.

In the forge, the fires burned steadily. Theo thought back to the time before he met Grank. Fire was a wild, fierce thing, feared by owls. And there it was now, tamed — tamed and ready to do his bidding. Several hammers of different sizes hung on the wall of the cave. Theo's blacksmithing skills had improved since he came to the tree. Beyond battle claws and coal buckets, he had made all sorts of new things: a shallow pan that caught rainwater for drinking, a gridiron for charring meat over an open flame, and his newest invention which he called a "smaka" — a device that could squeeze the juice from milkberries to make large quantities of the tea that all the owls had come to love. Theo surveyed his creations. *I have made good things*, he thought. *And I can still make more good things!* Was it not possible that he could create something that would help Ivar the knight feel whole again? He was heartened by this thought.

Theo cloistered himself in his forge and toiled night and day. Not once did he emerge to hunt, eat, or even speak. Grank was concerned about his former apprentice, but knew that the stubborn blacksmith would not be dissuaded from his endeavor. Realizing his protests would fall on deaf ear slits, Grank chose to help instead, by leaving freshly killed prey and milkberry tea outside the forge every night. And every night, he heard the *ting ting ting* of Theo's hammer and the hiss of steam as white-hot metal met cold water.

As the moon began its newing, Theo emerged from

Hammer and tongs

his forge, thin, tired, and covered in soot. What he had created was an iron foot. In shape, the iron foot looked astoundingly like a real owl's foot, only without feathers. You see, an owl's foot has four toes. In flight, we keep three toes facing forward, and one backward. When perched, or otherwise clutching something — a quill, an ice weapon, or freshly caught prey, the outer front toe on each foot pivots so that two toes face forward and two backward. Those of us who have studied owl anatomy can tell you that this is possible due to a flexible joint unique to owls. Theo was able to mimic this joint in iron with remarkable accuracy. Owls, like other birds of prey, have the ability to lock their toes around a perch. For the iron foot, Theo built a small latch that performed this function. It was easily activated with a tap of the beak. The top of the iron foot was fashioned into a narrow cup. Theo lined it first with lemming leather and then with soft down from his own chest. Attached to the cup were straps made from the sinews of prey. These would allow the iron foot to be fastened to Ivar's newly healed stump.

Theo set out to find Ivar at once.

Ivar had scarcely left his hollow since he was released by the healer. Many of Ivar's friends had tried to shake him out of his melancholy, but none had been successful. Lord Rathnik had all but given up on the young knight. Vreta had encouraged him to try to fly again, but he made only a half-gizzarded attempt at flapping his wings. He roosted day and night, turning away visitors. Despite his youth, his feathers had turned an ashen shade, his once-lustrous spots fading into the dull gray background. The owl that Theo set his eyes upon seemed to have aged years in the brief moon cycle since his encounter with the kraals.

"What's the use, Theo?" Ivar said drily. "I will never be a knight again. I wish you'd all stop fussing over me, and just leave me be."

"You'll always be recognized as a knight here. You don't have to fight to be a real owl. There are plenty of other things you can do." Theo pushed the iron foot toward Ivar. "This will help."

"Help? Help me look like a fool, perhaps."

This was not the reaction Theo had hoped for. "It will allow you to do more than *this*." He reminded himself to soften his tone. "You will be able to perch normally. And, in time, walk and —"

"What do you take me for? A *ground* animal? What good does walking do me? I will never be anything but a broken owl. I would have been better off dying with my comrades."

Theo could not hold back his anger. "I just thought that, maybe, you'd want to try to live your life again. That maybe you'd like to do the things that we owls do, to perch, to fly, and maybe even to hunt, or to —"

Ivar's yellow eyes brightened for the first time since his return to the tree. "Might I truly be able to . . . to *fly*?" The word "fly" came out of his beak in a bare whisper, as if saying it too loudly would quash the possibility.

Theo's gizzard quickened. "Yes, yes, I think so."

"Let's have a better look at this iron foot of yours, then."

Ivar would learn to fly a second time. And for the next moon cycle, he became a chick again — first learning to stand firmly on his new foot, learning to balance on a perch, and then to walk. The iron leg was heavy, and, despite Theo's crafty design, hard to control. Ivar had to regain his strength before he was capable of even attempting to branch. But with Theo as his tutor, Ivar grew closer to flight each night.

"It's an issue of balance. Remember when you first learned to fly with battle claws? It's like that, but just . . . well, more so. Let's begin with a simple glide." Theo and Ivar stood on a branch of the great tree. For the first time since his return, Ivar was about to take to the air.

"It *is* like a battle claw, isn't it? I'm ready."

Theo gave him a reassuring nod, and the Spotted Owl lifted off.

"Woah! Wooooah!" Ivar was in the air for no more than a few seconds before he started to stagger. Theo remembered how Grank had given him a little bit of a wing prop when he first learned to fly with battle claws. He did the same for Ivar by quickly flying under him and pumping his own wings to send up a few supportive puffs of air.

"Pump harder with your starboard wing! A little more. That's it, lift! Lift! Easy on the port side!"

"I'm doing it! I'm flying! Aiyee, I feel like an owlet again!" Although he was a bit unsteady, he was airborne. Ivar was ecstatic.

Theo was even more ecstatic. *He's flying! He is almost his old self again!* he thought. Somehow, seeing the once-broken knight in flight eased the regrets he had about making battle claws. His smithing had done something good for owlkind. His smithing had restored a young owl. Theo had been teaching many of the owls at the tree his art. Now, finally, he was sure that he was doing the right thing by passing his craft to the next generation.

Theo and Ivar became mentor and protégé. The two owls would practice together every night when the weather was clear and the winds not too blustery. Ivar's flight grew more and more stable. He was able to bank and dive with some training. He found landing to be surprisingly easy, as the weight of the iron foot actually made for a steadier approach. He began to work on catching prey — that took more coordination than he imagined. The one aspect of flight that eluded Ivar was endurance. Despite all his hard work, he could only fly for a few minutes at a time, usually circling the Island of Hoole. Never was he able to leave the air mass above the island for fear of losing altitude over water. That is, until Ivar made a curious finding.

Being a Spotted Owl, Ivar was particularly sensitive to changes in atmospheric pressure. Every night, as he circled the island with Theo, he noticed a slightly buoyant pocket of warm air as he passed over the southwestern coast. Whenever he was over this pocket, the iron foot's weight disappeared and he felt as though he had never lost it. He began to explore this pocket on his own. Sure enough, when he found its edges, he discovered that, if he stayed within them, he could fly for hours. It was as if he was back in his old fighting form again. One discovery led to another. As the months passed, Ivar explored farther and farther, finding more atmospheric anomalies around the island. With his iron foot, to which he was now fully accustomed, he drew diagrams of all of them. These charts were the first ever to be drawn in such detail.

"These are amazing!" Theo remarked over the charts that now numbered in the dozens. Ivar had asked Theo to meet him one evening in the great tree's new library. "You should show these to the chaw leaders. They might want to add these to our collection." Theo gestured to the growing stacks of books and maps around them.

"I'm no scholar." Ivar let out a modest chuckle. "I leave that to the likes of Strix Strumajen and her daughter. They have no need for a talzzard like me." Talzzard was a nickname that some of the fighter owls used to describe themselves — all talon and gizzard, and all fight.

"Seems to me that you're more than a talzzard now. I

think they might ask you to start sharing your discoveries with the rest of the tree." Theo was proud of the young Spotted Owl. Indeed, he had become so much more than he was before his injury. He was participating in as many chaw practices as he could fit into a given night. His enthusiasm had greatly impressed many of the chaw leaders.

"Maybe another night. I asked you here to show you this." Ivar pushed an unfinished chart toward Theo. Exactly what it showed, I cannot be sure. What I do know is that it showed some sort of air current. "It's unfinished because I had been afraid to fly farther west. I suspected that I might not make it back if I kept following it. Bucking this thermal stream would be grueling even for a very strong flier. But then I thought perhaps there is a windkin" — a windkin is a companion for another wind from an opposite quadrant; they work together in strange ways — "and if I could find the windkin for this one I might be able to fly to some faraway place."

"Fascinating! How will you know where this thermal stream, or its windkin as you call it, might lead? You must show this to Strix Strumajen. Maybe she can —"

"No. I want to fly it. Alone. I need to see where it leads, Theo."

Theo was taken aback. "You just said yourself that you think you might not make it back. This is an issue of safety."

"I can't worry about safety. I'm just going to follow it. And I mean to leave tonight."

"It's just, awfully impulsive, don't you think?" Theo remembered when Grank had accused *him* of being impulsive. That was so long ago. *Maybe impulse is one of those things that dwenks like the moon as an owl grows older.* He turned his attention back to the Spotted Owl.

"Maybe it will bring me back here one day, or maybe it won't. All those months ago, just before you brought me this iron foot, I thought that my days of adventuring were over, that my life was over. But you changed that. And I knew in my gizzard as soon as I took to the air that I had another long voyage in me." Ivar paused for a moment. "Something about being in that river of wind, feeling like I can fly forever, makes me feel whole again."

That, more than anything, touched Theo. To make Ivar whole again, wasn't that what he had set out to do? He was about to lose a friend, yes. But he was losing a friend to a fantastic voyage, not to war or violence. The gizzard-resister in him felt at peace for the first time since he strapped on battle claws. At last, he found balance in his heart and gizzard. Ivar began rolling up his charts, deftly using his iron foot in the process. Theo thought about making a comment about the foot, the charts, and this journey, but instead all he said was, "Glauxspeed, Ivar, Glauxspeed."

Theo left the tree shortly after Ivar's departure. Now, you must understand that in the legends, it was never clear where Theo went. For centuries, there were rumors that he finally joined the Glauxian Brothers, but no one knew for sure. Then there were other tales that intimated that Theo never joined the brothers and, in fact, followed Ivar. The recently discovered Theo Papers indeed prove this to be so. I am still in the process of translating them, and have yet to find out all the details of his life after he left the great tree, and his residence in what we now call the Sixth Kingdom. But I do know one thing — and that is that this Great Horned left behind an incredible legacy, not just of battle claws, but of creations that bettered owlkind. The Great Ga'Hoole Tree's loss was the Sixth Kingdom's gain.

A Year of Celebrations at the Great Tree

*I*n the world of owls, many holidays are celebrated and numerous festivals are held throughout the year. Some of these are boisterous and grand while others are solemn and intimate. Some are universally observed while others are unique to the Great Ga'Hoole Tree. We revel all night and into the day to mark those things that are most meaningful to us, for such is the way of owls.

FOUNDER'S NIGHT (OR LONG NIGHT)

Founder's Night is the first and last holiday of the owl year at the Great Ga'Hoole Tree. It begins at twilight on the shortest day of the year. Before Hoole came to power, Founder's Night was simply known as Long Night. Long Night had been one of the most festive holidays in the N'yrthghar, for it celebrated the disappearance of the sun and the longest darkness of the whole year. And in the universe of owls, where night is more valued than day, it became a festive time when young owls and older owls could fly to their gizzards' content and waste little time sleeping. The days would thereafter begin to lengthen and the long dark of the night would disappear sliver by sliver until, come summer, it would all begin to reverse again and there would be still another celebration on the shortest night to welcome back the darkness.

Shortly after the great tree was established, the owls of the tree renamed the holiday Founder's Night for their new king, Hoole, who was hatched on Long Night. Many owls from the Northern Kingdoms still refer to it as Long Night. Whatever you call it, it's the liveliest celebration of the year! There are all sorts of sports and games, and gad-feathers come to sing and do their lively sky jigs against the moon.

At First Lavender, throngs of owls emerge from their hollows and nests and take to the skies for a tween-time flight to kick off the celebration. This leads to the most exciting activity of the night — the flying contests. There's always a contest to see who's the fastest flier, of course. But we owls can get pretty creative when it comes to flying. I've seen (and even flown in a few) contests for the steepest dives, the sharpest turns, the fastest spirals, the most number of somersaults in a row, the tightest formations. . . . You name it, an owl has flown it. And if the conditions are right, there are colliering contests, too. Winners are greeted with roaring cheers and crowned with wreaths woven of humble materials such as vines and shoots of the Ga'Hoole tree. This reminds us of two things; that Hoole wore no crown of gold and needed no kingly trappings, and that each and every owl is noble in spirit if noble in deed.

Winner's wreath

There is also a hunting contest to celebrate the spirit of lochinvyrr, taught to Hoole in his day and Coryn in ours by the dire wolves of Beyond the Beyond. Only a few owls, the best hunters, are selected to participate. Owls compete to see who gets the quickest kill, the largest prey, and the quietest approach. When the hunters bring back their prey, they are greeted with much gratitude. Following the hunting contest, there is a great feast. The raw prey is shared by all to remind us that we have been able to survive only through the sharing of resources.

As the night goes on, owls return to the sky for more dancing and fancy flying. By daybreak, most owls are exhausted and return to their nests and hollows for a most restful day of sleep.

OWLIPOPPEN FESTIVAL

The Owlipoppen Festival takes place on the night of the first full moon after Founder's Night. It's a minor festival, but also one of the oldest. I have loved going to this festival ever since I was an owlet. And even though I am a fully fledged owl, a ryb at the great tree no less, I have never ceased to get a thrill out of seeing all those colorful owlipoppen. While I am usually not a fan of ostentatious displays, this festival is just so full of history and artistic expression that I cannot help but love it.

In this festival, elaboratly decorated owlipoppen — little owl dolls made from down, molted feathers, and sometimes twigs — are loaded up on makeshift rafts and sent out to sea with the tide with the wish that they take with them any bad luck for the coming year.

This festival is steeped in tradition. It began in the coastal regions of the Southern Kingdoms thousands of years ago as a cleansing ritual. Originally, owls would gather their molted feathers and rub them all over themselves. Misfortune was thought to have been transferred to the feathers. The feathers would then be cast off into the sea, and the owl would have nothing but good luck throughout the year. Soon, owls who lived along rivers began to pick up the custom as well, sending their molted feathers downriver.

This ritual evolved into the making of owlipoppen. These days, owls sometimes begin making the elaborate dolls weeks before the festival. They are often much fancier than the owlipoppen that parents make for their chicks. Feathers are dyed using the juices from berries and grasses. And if there are owlets in the family, they help to decorate the finished dolls with leaves, nuts, and small stones. The night before the festival, owls gather to make a raft. They tie sticks and twigs together with dried vines to make a large floating platform for the owlipoppen.

On the night of the festival, all the owls in the community bring their owlipoppen to the shore and place them on the raft. Everyone admires the other owlipoppen and sings the "Good Luck Song" together. I had been fairly certain that the song is a recent addition to the festival. My research proved me right — it was written and first sung by Madame Uli Plonk, a singer at the great tree only two centuries ago.

Owlipoppen

Luck be in my feathers, sorrows I untether
Luck be in my feathers for all that I will weather

Gather at the waters
Owls of all the land
All my sons and daughters
Let ill omens be banned

Come sing a joyful note
To help improve our lot

Sorrows that yonder float
Shall quickly be forgot

Let the owlipoppen drift
Toward the light of dawn
In waters that run swift
Our fortunes be redrawn

Luck be in my feathers, sorrows I untether
Luck be in my feathers for all that I will weather

When the tide is right, the owl who has been designated as "Lucky Owl" for the festival (usually some sort of community leader), pushes the raft into the sea or river. As the owlipoppen float out over the water, all the owls who have gathered take to the skies and hoot and holler as loudly as they can to give any bad luck a proper send-off. The night ends with the choosing of the Lucky Owl for next year's Owlipoppen Festival.

EGG FESTIVAL

The Egg Festival takes place on the first equal-night of the year, when the length of the day is the same as the length of the night. It is the night that marks the beginning of spring — one of the most important times of the year for owls, for it is the time when most eggs are laid and the next generation comes into being. The Egg Festival celebrates this process.

This is not a festival full of feasts and gatherings as some others are. It is one that is observed unfussily. Nevertheless, it is full of significance for owlkind.

Rituals vary from region to region and from species to species. Calling songs are always sung. Each species has its own unique call. Spotted Owls, for example, issue a series of short, barking hoots, whereas Barn Owls emit long, drawn-out shrieks. As the night falls, and the Egg Festival begins, a symphony of calls can be heard in every place where owls live. Some owls also put egg-shaped stones in their nests to symbolize their wish for a brood of healthy, robust chicks.

SCROOMSAWIKKEN

To owls, death is believed to be the passage to another life in glaumora. It's not necessarily scary or sad, but merely a journey that we must all embark upon. Scroomsawikken has been celebrated since the time of the legends as a night when the living remember and honor their departed loved ones.

Traditionally, on the night of Scroomsawikken, on the first new moon after spring's equal night, the mood is bright and not at all gruesome. It's treated almost like a family reunion of sorts. The deceased are remembered fondly. Owls return to the site of their loved ones' final ceremonies to pay respects. Some owls offer flowers, others bits of food and furs to make the departed ones' stay in glaumora more comfortable. Often, there is singing and dancing at the sites, for owls want to bring joy to the ones they love, even after death.

At the great tree, owls light candles in the Great Hollow to pay tribute to the deceased. Every year, I light a candle for Strix Struma. Now, with the passing of Ezylryb, Boron, and Barran, there are so many more candles to light. Each point of light reminds me what amazing owls they all were, and how they're surely making glaumora an even better place.

NIMSY NIGHT

Nimsy Night takes place on the shortest night of the year and marks the start of summer. Owls see it as an occasion for welcoming back the darkness, for after Nimsy Night, the nights grow steadily longer until the arrival of Founder's Night (Long Night). It is also the time to usher in the warmest months of the year, when prey is plentiful and flying is most pleasant.

During the time of the Golden Rain at the great tree, chaw practices are cut short, young owls take fewer classes, and all owls enjoy as many night flights as they can possibly fit into the few hours of darkness. So, all the owls look forward to the coming of Nimsy Night because it signals the change to a more leisurely schedule. I, of course, always seem to work just as hard as I do the rest of the year.

Everything is decorated with the color green for Nimsy Night. The leaves of maples, oaks, and sycamores reach a bright, verdant shade during this time of year. So owls string them together to make garlands and wreaths. These are placed over hollows and nests, and are said to bring good fortune and health. Some owls even dye their primaries green in celebration.

The best-known ritual of Nimsy Night is the picking of herbs. Since ancient times, owls have believed that herbs are at their most potent and have miraculous healing powers on the shortest night of the year. Therefore, we pick them on this night to dry and use throughout the year. Now, I don't think this is a scientifically proven fact, so I question its validity. But, herbs do seem to be most abundant in early summer, so I suppose it's only sensible to gather them at this time.

And as with all great celebrations in the world of owls, there is a feast associated with Nimsy Night. It's not quite as grand as the feasts for Founder's Night or the Milkberry Harvest Festival, but it's wonderful nonetheless. Families of owls gather to share meat, which is plentiful at this time of year.

At the great tree, there is traditionally a snail bake. Raw snails are not the tastiest of foods for owls — most of us find them too slimy. But once they're cooked, they become an absolute delicacy! A typical snail bake begins with the heating of great stones near the shoreline. The colliering and metals chaws are responsible for this. Coals are buried among the stones early in the evening, so that at feast time, they are good and hot. Next comes the gathering of fresh seaweed — the southern coast of the Island of Hoole is especially good for this. This is usually a job for the larger owls, as the seaweed can be quite heavy. In the meantime, smaller owls gather snails from around the island. This is very easy after a rain, and somewhat more challenging when the weather has been fair. The snails are thrown onto the stones followed by the seaweed and a few of the herbs picked earlier in the night. The sound of snail shells hitting hot stones is always met with a great cheer. Then, the whole thing is covered in sand to trap the heat. After an hour or two, when the snails have cooked and the fire cooled, the sand and seaweed are removed and the eating begins! The snail bake always reminds me how lucky I am to live at the tree — where a little ingenuity and the ability to control fire combine to create an exquisite treat out of otherwise lowly fare.

MOON FESTIVAL

The eighth full moon of the owl year is said to be the brightest and the roundest. And it is during this time that we owls celebrate the Moon Festival, when families come together, even from the farthest reaches of the owl kingdoms.

The Moon Festival is founded on legend. It is said that there were once three moons in the sky that lit up the night as bright as day. And in the Shadow Forest lived an owl named Vilis, who was the best flier in all the land. He had a beautiful mate named Ilona, who loved him. After many happy years together, Vilis and Ilona grew old. Vilis found that other owls, younger owls, now flew faster and higher than he. He was chagrined, and vowed that he would not accept his fate. He sought out the mage of the forest, a spider named Zuzanna. "Zuzanna, make me fly as strongly as I did when I was a young owl," he begged. "I'll do anything you ask in return."

"Three moons are too bright for me. I think one will suit me just fine. Bring down two of the moons, and everlasting youth and strength shall be yours," Zuzanna ordered him.

"How can I accomplish such a thing? 'Tis an impossible task," Vilis complained.

"My magical elixir will help you to accomplish your task. When I see only one moon in the sky, I will give you more of the elixir, and you will be made young once again. But be warned, the elixir is only to be taken by he who brings down the moons."

Vilis agreed.

Zuzanna instructed Vilis to take ten drops of the elixir, which gave him the strength of a thousand owls. He flew all the way to one of the moons, grabbed it with his talons, and dragged it toward Earth. He plunged it into the sea, darkening the night sky. He flew to another of the moons and did the same. Now there was only one moon in the sky, and the night was as dark as it is today.

Zuzanna gave Vilis more of her magical elixir as she had promised, and instructed him to take only one drop a year. The single drop gave Vilis the strength of his youth, and once again, Vilis was the strongest flier in all the land.

A youthful Vilis greeted Ilona when he finally returned home. She was becoming a withered old owl with white feathers and weak wings. This made her sad. She did not want to be old and feeble while her mate appeared to be in the prime of his life. So, one night, while Vilis was out hunting, she sought out her mate's magical elixir, hoping that it would make her young as well. Having no knowledge of Zuzanna's instructions, Ilona took a small swallow from the vial. She could feel the power of the elixir coursing through her, and her feathers regained their color and luster. Thrilled, she flew out of her hollow to find her mate.

But Ilona would never find Vilis again. With just a few wing flaps, she flew all the way to the last moon in the sky. There, the elixir lost its effect, as Zuzanna had divined its misuse. Ilona was trapped on the moon with no way to go home.

Vilis returned to his hollow to find his mate gone. Months passed and she did not come back. Desperate, he returned to Zuzanna for help. Zuzanna told him of his mate's trespass. She decreed that, as punishment for taking the elixir without permission, Ilona would not be allowed to return to Earth ever again. Vilis was devastated and began to cry. Zuzanna felt pity for the owl who had darkened the sky for her. So, she granted Vilis the opportunity to go to the moon once a year to visit his mate. The two lovers are reunited on the eighth full moon every year, and that is why the moon glows the brightest on this night.

On the night of the Moon Festival, families gather to admire the moon together, sing moon songs, and eat round moon cakes made with nuts and berries. As the full moon begins to dwenk, young owls light lanterns to show Vilis the way back to Earth.

MILKBERRY HARVEST FESTIVAL

The Milkberry Harvest Festival is a singularly Ga'Hoolian festival. At the Great Ga'Hoole Tree, the four seasons are named after the colors of the milkberry vines that cascade from every branch. Winter is the time of the White Rain, spring is the time of the Silver Rain, summer is the time of the Golden Rain, and autumn is the time of the Copper-

Rose Rain. During the time of the Copper-Rose Rain, the milkberries are the ripest and plumpest for picking. The delicious berries of the vines make up a major part of our non-meat diet. Ripe berries are crushed and brewed into tea. They're also made into delicious stews, cakes, and loaves of fragrant bread. The dried berries are used for snacks, for they are highly nutritious and a source of instant energy. Milkberries are as Ga'Hoolian as Hoole himself. This is why the Milkberry Harvest Festival is one of the grandest festivals of the year.

Milkberries

The harvest begins on the second equal night of the year. All classes and chaw practices are canceled for seven days. Even daytime sleep is shortened. For the first three days, the owls at the tree help harvest all the berries and trim the vines. Then, on the third night, the real festivities begin. There is a banquet to celebrate a successful harvest, which goes on for the next three to four nights. The Great Hollow is festooned with cut vines and berries. Candles make the entire tree glow against the night sky. A huge assortment of milkberry treats are made and eaten. There is joyous dancing and singing all over the Island of Hoole. And more often than not, the older owls get tipsy on milkberry wine and berry mead. During the height of the celebration, owls forgo sleep for as long as they can. But with all the wine, mead, and dancing, a few inevitably pass out before the party is over.

PUNKIE NIGHT

A favorite holiday for fledglings, Punkie Night takes place on the night of the first new moon after the Milkberry Festival. It is a night filled with sweets and mischief.

Young owls make and wear masks that make them look like other species of owls, or even other birds. When Great Grays don Pygmy Owl masks and vice versa, they always get hoots of laughter. While wearing these masks, young owls fly from hollow to hollow, offering songs and dances in return for blessings and gifts of sweets. This is called "galooshing." Most of the time, owls give out dried berries and such, but if you are lucky, you might find a hollow that gives out nootie tarts or pine-nut cakes. Of course, you have to work extra hard to earn the *good* sweets. For my first Punkie Night, I wanted to be something really special. So, I did lots of research on rare owl species, and made myself a *Magascops ingens*, or Rufescent Screech Owl, mask. Well, to my disappointment, nobody got it. After that, I stuck to bird species that everyone would recognize.

After galooshing, young owls gather for sweet-swapping and games. Everyone tries to trade loads of the ordinary treats for a few of the good ones. But, to each his own, I suppose — for every owl who hates dried caterpillars, there's inevitably one who loves them. One of the most popular Punkie Night games at the great tree is Blooking for Milkberries. The name of the game comes from the sound that owlets make when they plunge their faces into the water — *blook blook*. Even owlets who have yet to fledge can join in the fun. Milkberries float in a large bucket of water, and blindfolded participants must use their beaks to pick up a berry.

Sometimes, young owls like to play tricks on the grown-ups on Punkie Night — putting sap in their nests, tying their talons together with vine while they sleep, those types of vile tricks. After more than one post-Punkie

Night's rest, I have found myself feather-stuck to my nest. I must say that I do *not* approve of this type of uncouth behavior on Punkie Night — or any other night for that matter.

After the festivities are over, older owls often try to tell the fledglings to ration their treats. But as a matter of course, the young'uns go to sleep the next morning with bellies that ache from too many sweets.

BALEFIRE NIGHT

Balefire Night celebrates the Guardians' command of fire. Since the time of the legends, we have used fire to make tools and weapons, to cook food, and to cast light where light is needed. During the last fine days of the Copper-Rose Rain, owls come together to light the night up as bright as day with a bonfire.

Owls dance around the bonfire, first circling it tightly; then, as the fire burns hotter, the circles grow wider and wider. The more adventurous owls will also fly directly above the bonfire to ride the intense thermal drafts.

As the fire dies down, owls use the hot coals to roast meat and nooties. At the great tree, only cooked meat is eaten on Balefire Night. This is to celebrate the Ga'Hoolian tradition of using fire to alter food. Most owls eat their meat raw and bloody — there is nothing wrong with this, of course. In fact, I still enjoy the occasional fur-on-meat, freshly caught. As our beloved Ezylryb once said, "You've gotta throw some fur in there for ballast before flying into a hurricane." But the heat lends the food a certain something. I still remember the first time I tried cooked meat as a young owl. It was as if that roasted bat awakened a part of my gizzard that I didn't know existed.

At the end of the night, coals from the bonfire are retrieved by colliers and brought to the forge to be used on another night.

Nooties

Night and Day at the Great Tree

At the great tree, all owls, especially the young ones, follow a set schedule. There is a time for study and practice, a time for hunting and eating, and a time for simply gleeking about.

An owl's night begins at First Lavender, when the sun begins to dip beneath the horizon and the sky turns a pale blue laced with streaks of purple and pink. Each owl has his or her wake-up routine. This usually involves preening, combing the head with claws, ruffling up plumage, and cleaning claws and toes by nibbling with the beak. This is also the time that the singer of the tree sings her first song of the night, "Evensong." It is gentle but invigorating, and I have never tired of hearing it.

At tween time, or twilight, the tree really begins to bustle. Many species of owls hunt as twilight descends, since many kinds of prey are active at this time. At the tree, some owls prefer to wait until tweener for their first meal while others inevitably wake up starving and take to the skies immediately to find a plump bat or vole.

The earliest, not to mention most dreaded, classes and chaw practice begin at tween time. I, for one, believe that it's good for the head and the gizzard to begin the night early, and so, I have scheduled all my introductory Ga'Hoolology classes for this time. The young ones might gripe now, but they'll thank me later. Not all owls have class or chaw practice at tween time, it all depends on your schedule, of course. Those who have free time may choose to spend it in flight or in study at the library. Would you believe that some owls actually sleep in when they don't have early classes? Appalling behavior, if you ask me, leads to laziness and foggy thinking.

Nightfall is called First Black, for the last tinges of gray fade from the sky and it turns the color of cold coal. This is when owls begin gathering in the dining hollow for tweener, the first meal of the day served at the great tree. The nest-maids of the Great Ga'Hoole Tree serve as dining tables for the owls, each snake stretching herself to accommodate at least a half dozen of us. Acorn porridge, roasted tree slugs, grilled bats, and braised mice are all tweener favorites. And there's always milkberry tea — served piping hot in nut cups.

Chaw practice and classes resume after tweener. I should mention that chaw practices don't occur exclusively at night. Sometimes, chaw work requires that you practice in the middle of the day when one would otherwise be sleeping. I remember being pulled out of a lovely slumber to see a forest fire when I was first tapped for the weather-interpretation and colliering chaws. Directly following tweener parliament has its regular meetings. They don't convene every night, but there is always a lot of business to discuss. Important matters sometimes make themselves known in the middle of the day and cannot wait until the next scheduled meeting. Many parliament meetings have occurred during the bright of day.

Nut cups

One of my favorite times of night at the great tree is teatime. It gives the body and mind a chance to rest after working and studying hard. Milkberry tea has long been a staple at the tree. Many chaw practices and mission strategies have been discussed while sipping the brew in the dining hollow. On a cold night, a hot cup puts a little extra fluff in your feathers. And on a hot day, it's the most refreshing way to refuel. To make this, the most Ga'Hoolian of beverages, the cook procures the ripest milkberries available. A smaka, an invention of Theo's that has changed little in a thousand years, is used to crush the berries into pulp. Hot water and some mint leaves are added to the pulp, and the mixture steeps in a large bucket for several minutes. Finally, the mixture is strained into teapots. In the summertime, the tea is often chilled in the root cellar before it is served. Along with milkberry tea, nootie cakes, milkberry tarts, and berry bread are served at teatime. These are specialties of the tree that I have almost never had outside of our little island.

The darkest time of night comes after teatime. This is when most introductory navigation classes are held, for it's when the stars glow the brightest against the black sky. It is also the perfect time for night flight. There isn't any special purpose to night flight. It really is mostly recreational. As Boron once told me, newly arrived owls are encouraged to buddy up with other young owls at the tree to "tell a few jokes, yarp a few pellets, and hoot at the moon." Sometimes, however, young owls have to forego night flight to finish their homework or study for a test the next evening. No owl likes to give up night flight, but such is the way of the scholar.

Breaklight, the last meal of the night, is eaten at Deep Gray, a short time before dawn. Owls gather in the dining hollow once more for a light meal of raw or roasted meat, insects, and even spiders and frogs. Some owls skip break-light altogether, preferring to hunt during night flight. But even those owls like to go to the dining hollow to share a pot of tea and partake in good conversation.

Just as tween time is the twilight between sunset and night, twixt time is what we owls call the twilight between night and dawn, when the sun has not yet risen above the horizon, but the sky to the east is tinged with orange and blue. The singer sings "Night Is Done," the goodlight song, to signal that it is once again time to roost. Owls retreat to their hollows to sleep in nests lined with the finest mosses and fluffiest down. Many young owls these days will tell you of how they've drifted off to sleep day after day to the sound of Madame Plonk's voice and the music of the great grass harp. Others will tell you that nothing feels more tranquil than watching the sun peek over the horizon at First Light.

As the daylight embraces the Island of Hoole, some owls pause to give thanks to Glaux, others reflect on the events of the previous night and make plans for the next night, while still others turn to their books and study just a little bit longer before going to sleep. In the hours when the sun shines its brightest, the owls of the great tree slumber. The next night, they begin their routines once again. May Glaux bless this cycle, night after night.

A Few Final Words . . .

My dear scholars of Ga'Hoole, it is my heartfelt wish that this humble volume has adequately guided you on your journey through the world of Ga'Hoole. This is but a small slice of life at the great tree — there are still stories that remain untold and great owls whom you have barely gotten to know. But I hope that what you have read has endeared you to the principles that make our tree great. May it inspire you all to band together wherever you are and do good and noble deeds in the spirit of the Great Ga'Hoole Tree.

Just a Few More Final Words . . .

I must take this opportunity to thank my two most diligent assistants, Calista and Bax. I know I tend to become rather . . . prolix when it comes to the subjects I love. As such, I have gained the unfortunate reputation of being a tad long-winded. Thankfully, Calista and Bax were there to curb my enthusiasm. They were also indispensable when it came to the wealth of research that this project demanded.

I would also like to thank Rikard, the talented young artist of the tree who has lent the skills of his talon for the illustrations in this volume. He has given the book a most artful touch. Rikard, at the urging of Calista and Bax, painted the portrait of yours truly found at the front of this book. Normally, I would have objected to such a display, but all three of them insisted on it — for posterity, they said. I could not argue.

Finally, I must tell you, dear scholars, that as I wrote this guide book to the great tree, I had the uncanny feeling that I was being guided by a kindred spirit — the spirit of an Other from a distant time and place. Even in sleep this illusion pursued me, and one day after I had worked on this tome long into midday and fell asleep at my scribblings, head on wing, a name came to me in my dreams, a strange, sonorous name. Kathryn Huang. Strange, is it not?

Hoo's Hoo of Ga'Hoole

The Band

SOREN: Male Barn Owl (*Tyto alba*). The second son of Noctus and Marella, Soren was hatched in his family's fir tree nest in the Forest Kingdom of Tyto. Before he could fly, Soren was pushed from his nest by his brother, Kludd, as a part of a disturbing initiation ceremony performed by the Pure Ones. Helpless on the forest floor, Soren was snatched by patrolling owls from St. Aegolius Academy for Orphaned Owls. There, he met his best friend, Gylfie, and the two made a desperate attempt for freedom. Soren, along with the rest of the Band, sought out the Great Ga'Hoole Tree. And, indeed, it was Soren's destiny to become a Guardian of Ga'Hoole. With his strong gizzard and natural colliering abilities, Soren was tapped for the colliering and weather-interpretation chaws. Since then, he has flown many missions and fought in many battles.

Most notably, he spearheaded the rescue effort of Ezlryb, his venerated mentor, from a devious trap set by Kludd and his followers. The following winter, he and Gylfie led a group of owls in an undercover mission to infiltrate St. Aggie's. He was also a hero in the Battle of Fire and Ice, when the Guardians attacked the Pure Ones' stronghold.

GYLFIE: Female Elf Owl (*Micranthene whitneyi*). Gylfie is from the Desert Kingdom of Kuneer. At the age of three weeks, she made a mistake that thousands of young owlets have made — she tried to fly before she was ready. Like Soren, she was snatched and imprisoned at St. Aegolius Academy for Orphaned Owls. After she arrived at the tree with the Band, she was tapped for the navigation chaw. Quick-witted and resourceful, she proved to be a great asset to the prestigious elite fighting-and-mission group known as the Chaw of Chaws. Her extensive vocabulary makes her the most eloquent speaker of the group.

TWILIGHT: Male Great Gray Owl (*Strix nebulosa*). Twilight is a free flier — having brought himself up without the civilizing effects of parents, he is very independent and something of a rough character. Hatched in the moments just after the sun dips below the horizon but the darkness has yet to set in, he has the uncanny ability to see in the murky grayness that is tween time. He is a fearless owl who has a good heart and is an invaluable ally in any fight. His fighting skills are equaled only by his lingual dexterity. He can be your best friend or your worst enemy. Twilight is a member of the search-and-rescue chaw and the Chaw of Chaws. It was he who gave the final death blow to Kludd, sparing his friend Soren from the atrocious act of fratricide.

DIGGER: Male Burrowing Owl (*Athene cunicularia*, formerly *Speotyto cunicularius*). Digger is from the Desert Kingdom of Kuneer. He met the rest of the Band when he was wandering alone, lost in the desert after an attack by a St. Aegolius patrol in which his brother was killed. Quiet and contemplative, Digger is the philosopher of the Band. He is a member of the tracking chaw as well as the Chaw of Chaws.

Owls of the Great Ga'Hoole Tree

CORYN: Male Barn Owl (*Tyto alba*). Born on the night of an eclipse, Nyroc was the much-awaited son of Nyra and Kludd. From birth he was strictly trained, under Nyra, to become High Tyto, leader of the Pure Ones. However, his destiny was to know the paths of both good and evil, and to choose one. At that choosing, he rejected the evil ways of the Pure Ones and renamed himself Coryn. He went on to retrieve the powerful Ember of Hoole from the Northern Kingdoms and claim his place at the Great Ga'Hoole Tree as its rightful king.

OTULISSA: Female Spotted Owl (*Strix occidentalis*). Writer, ryb, collier, weathertrix, and consummate scholar, Otulissa is an owl of all trades. She is a direct descendant of the famous weathertrix Strix Emerilla. She has a strong academic bent and is the repository of much knowledge, not all of it useful. She is a loyal friend to those dear to her, and can be lethal in close combat. Her learning makes her an essential member of the Chaw of Chaws. She also has played a crucial role in the education of young Coryn.

MARTIN: Male Northern Saw-whet Owl (*Aegolius acadicus*). As a young student at the great tree, Martin was double chawed with Soren and Otulissa in weather interpretation and colliering. His small stature belies his prowess in battles and on missions. He is a member of the Chaw of Chaws.

RUBY: Female Short-eared Owl (*Asio flammeus*). Ruby lost her family under mysterious circumstances and was brought to the Great Ga'Hoole Tree at a young age. She is perhaps the best flier of all the owls at the tree, and easily became an expert weather interpreter and collier. She is also a member of the Chaw of Chaws.

EGLANTINE: Female Barn Owl (*Tyto alba*). Soren and Kludd's younger sister, Eglantine was brought to the tree during the Great Downing. At the tree, she was reunited with Soren and Mrs. Plithiver. As she was recovering, she came under the malign influence of Ginger, a refugee from the Pure Ones, and became shattered. In a courageous attempt to save the tree from danger, she stole, but then accidentally broke, Nyra's first egg.

PRIMROSE: Female Pygmy Owl (*Glaucidium californicum*). Primrose was rescued from a forest fire and brought to the Great Ga'Hoole Tree the same night that Soren and the Band arrived. When Eglantine was rescued in the Great Downing, Primrose quickly became her best friend. Though small in size, she showed great daring and courage as she discovered the reason for Eglantine's strange behavior — and saved Eglantine and the tree.

BORON: (*deceased*) Male Snowy Owl (*Bubo scandiacus*, formerly *Nyctea scandiaca*). Even though many owls referred to Boron as the King of Hoole, he was, in reality, the last steward of the great tree. Boron, along with his mate, Barran, acted as the head of the Hoolian parliament of owls.

BARRAN: (*deceased*) Female Snowy Owl (*Bubo scandiacus*, formerly *Nyctea scandiaca*). Often referred to as the Queen of Hoole, Barran was a kind and wise leader. She was also a distinguished search-and-rescue ryb. She, along with Boron, passed away shortly before the arrival of Coryn, the true king.

EZYLRYB: (*deceased*) Male Whiskered Screech Owl (*Megascops trichopsis*, formerly *Otus trichopsis*). Ezylryb was the wise and intrepid weather-interpretation and colliering ryb at the Great Ga'Hoole Tree. He was born Lyze of Kiel. Before coming to the Great Tree, Ezylryb fought in the War of the Ice Claws in which he was severely wounded and lost his beloved mate, Lil. After the war, he retreated in grief from worldly affairs. He spent many seasons at the Glauxian Brothers' retreat, where he studied weather and colliering extensively, finally leaving to pass on all he had learned to the owls at the great tree. He was Soren's mentor and considered him a son.

STRIX STRUMA: (*deceased*) Female Spotted Owl (*Strix occidentalis*). The dignified navigation ryb at the Great Ga'Hoole Tree, Strix Struma was fierce in battle and led a crack group of fighters known as Struma's Strikers. She had a proud and ancient lineage and was a well-respected veteran of the Battle of Little Hoole. She was struck down in the ferocious fighting against the Pure Ones during the Battle of the Siege.

SYLVANA: Female Burrowing Owl (*Athene cunicularia*, formerly *Speotyto cunicularius*). Sylvana is the young tracking ryb at the Great Ga'Hoole Tree. By all accounts, she is a very good teacher.

MADAME PLONK: Female Snowy Owl (*Bubo scandiacus*, formerly *Nyctea scandiaca*). Madame Brunwella Plonk is the elegant singer of the Great Ga'Hoole Tree. She comes from a long line of Snowies from the Plonk family who are famous for their beautiful voices. She is an owl in thrall of bright geegaws and enjoys the fineries offered by Trader Mags.

BUBO: Male Great Horned Owl (*Bubo virginianus*). Bubo is the blacksmith and the metals ryb at the Great Ga'Hoole Tree. He is often described as unusually large for a Great Horned Owl. He has been a great friend and confidant to Soren. His greatest invention has been the NAST (Nickel Alloy Super Talons).

Other Friendly Owls

HORTENSE (also known as Mist): Female Spotted Owl (*Strix occidentalis*). Hortense was snatched at an early age from her home in the Kingdom of Ambala by a St. Aegolius patrol. At St. Aggie's, she attempted to subvert the oppressive system by rescuing and restoring stolen eggs, and aiding Soren and Gylfie in their escape. Soren and Gylfie witnessed what they believed to be her death, but later discovered that she did not die, and is one and the same as the mysterious owl called Mist now living with the eagles Streak and Zan.

THE ROGUE SMITH OF SILVERVEIL: (*deceased*) Female Snowy Owl (*Bubo scandiacus*, formerly *Nyctea scandiaca*). Sister of the very refined Madame Plonk, and one of many scattered blacksmiths not attached to any kingdom in the owl world, she lived and worked alone in Silverveil. She became a valuable ally to the Guardians when she provided them with information about the Pure Ones.

SIMON: (*deceased*) Male Brown Fish Owl (*Bubo zeylonensis*, formerly *Ketupa zeylonensis*). A pilgrim owl of the Glauxian Brothers of the Northern Kingdoms, and sworn to help all those in need, Simon unwittingly nursed Kludd back to health after he was badly injured. An ungrateful and diabolical Kludd then turned on his caregiver and murdered the kindly Simon.

CLEVE OF FIRTHMORE: Male Spotted Owl (*Strix occiden-talis*). Cleve is a member of the noble family of Krakor and a student of medicine at the Glauxian Brothers' retreat in the Northern Kingdoms. Upon meeting Cleve, Otulissa felt her gizzard go a-twittering. She was quite taken with the dashing, noble Cleve — until she learned he was a pacifist.

DUSTYTUFT: (*deceased*). Male Greater Sooty Owl (*Tyto tene-bricosa*). Dustytuft, like all Sooties, was a low caste member of the Pure Ones. He bemoaned his fate of always being given the worst, dirtiest chores to do, until he was singled out by Nyra, and chosen to become the special friend of Nyroc, future High Tyto. He learned too late the horrifying purpose of this special friendship that was encouraged by Nyra. Dustytuft is also known, by Phillip.

GRIMBLE: (*deceased*). Male Boreal Owl (*Aegolius funerus*). Grimble was captured as an adult by the St. Aggie's patrols. He did not want to cooperate with their oppressive regime, but the leaders of St. Aggie's threatened his family with capture — or worse — if he did not lend his considerable muscle and fighting skills to their schemes. He rose to heroism when he aided Soren and Gylfie in their escape by teaching them how to fly.

TWILLA: Female Short-eared Owl (*Asio flammeus*). Once a skog, Twilla lost her entire clan during the War of the Ice Claws, and became a Glauxian Sister. She was acting as an attendant for Ifghar when she met Gylfie and Otulissa at the Glauxian Brothers' retreat. She rescued Gylfie from kraals in the Northern Kingdoms when they had captured the Elf Owl to gather information about the Guardians' planned invasion of the Pure Ones' stronghold.

GWYNDOR: Male Masked Owl (*Tyto novaehollandiae*). Gwyndor was a Rogue Smith summoned by the Pure Ones for the Marking Ceremony over Kludd's bones. Upon meeting Nyroc, the wise Rogue Smith suspected the young owl had firesight, and was destined for a future much different than that planned for him by his mother.

Snakes and Other Birds

MRS. PLITHIVER: A blind snake, "Mrs. P.," as Soren calls her, was formerly the nest-maid for Soren's family. When Soren made the journey to the great tree, he brought Mrs. Plithiver with him. She is now a member of the harp guild there and has attained the rarefied position of sliptween.

OCTAVIA: A Kielian snake, Octavia is the nest-maid for Madame Plonk, and was for Ezylryb when he was alive.

She came to the tree with Ezylryb after the War of the Ice Claws in which she was blinded. She knew Ezylryb and his difficult history better than anyone else. She is also a member of the prestigious harp guild.

HOKE OF HOCK: A Kielian snake, Hoke of Hock is the retired supreme commander of the stealth unit of the fighting snakes of the Kielian League. He flew with Lil, Ezylryb's mate, during the War of the Ice Claws. He proved to be a great ally to the Guardians as they prepared for their invasion of the Pure Ones' stronghold.

TRADER MAGS: Trader Mags is a Magpie and a traveling merchant — part tramp, part collector, and all original. She gathers and trades scraps of fabric, bits of broken crockery, crystals from broken chandeliers, books (whole or in part), bright pieces of stained glass — in short, anything pretty — from the ruins of the mysterious vanished race known only as the Others.

STREAK and ZAN: Hortense could not have saved all those eggs from St. Aggie's had it not been for the help of a pair of bald eagles named Streak and Zan. After Hortense's fall from the cliffs of St. Aggie's, it was Streak who caught her. He and Zan then nursed her back to health.

Known Enemies

IFGHAR: Male Whiskered Screech Owl (*Megascops trichopsis*, formerly *Otus trichopsis*). Ifghar is the younger brother of Ezylryb. During the War of the Ice Claws, he betrayed the Kielian League and became a turnfeather. Ifghar was hounded for his traitorous behavior, and long after his brother's departure was accepted as a refugee at the Glauxian Retreat. He is accompanied by Gragg, a Kielian snake, who is bound in service by loyalty to him.

DEWLAP: Female Burrowing Owl (*Athene cunicularia*, formerly *Speotyto cunicularius*). Once the Ga'Hoolology ryb at the Great Ga'Hoole Tree, Dewlap had deep respect for the history of the great tree and would have done anything to preserve it. Unfortunately, she made a traitorous choice that imperiled the tree and all the owls in it. Consequently, she was exiled to the Glauxian Sisters' retreat.

Leaders of St. Aegolius Academy
for Orphaned Owls

SKENCH: (*deceased*) Female Great Horned Owl (*Bubo virginianus*). Skench was the tyrannical Ablah General of St. Aegolius Academy for Orphaned Owls, a place where young owls were moon blinked and trained to forget their homes, their families, and their own true selves. She was forced to join forces with the Guardians when St. Aggie's was taken over by the Pure Ones.

SPOORN: (*deceased*) Male Western Screech Owl (*Megascops kennicottii*, formerly *Otus kennicottii*). Spoorn was the first lieutenant to Skench, and second in command at St. Aggie's.

The Pure Ones

KLUDD: (*deceased*) Barn Owl (*Tyto alba*). Kludd was Soren and Eglantine's older brother. From birth, he was fascinated by power and was soon attracted to a group calling themselves the Pure Ones. The Pure Ones believed that Barn Owls were a superior species of owls, and that Barn Owls had been granted by nature the right to rule, tyrannically, over all the other species of owls. He was killed by Twilight in a fierce fight during the Guardians' invasion of the Pure Ones' stronghold.

NYRA: Barn Owl (*Tyto alba*). Nyra was Kludd's mate. After Kludd's death, she took control of the Pure Ones and imparted her viciousness to all her followers. She is the mother of Nyroc/Coryn, whom she intended to groom into the perfect Pure One, a new High Tyto. But her son proved to be a poor student of evil. Coryn recently revealed that he suspects his mother is a hagsfiend.

WORTMORE: Barn Owl (*Tyto alba*). Wortmore is a Pure Guard lieutenant. He follows orders no matter how foul.

STRYKER: Barn Owl (*Tyto alba*). Stryker is a Pure One lieutenant major under Nyra.

UGLAMORE: (*deceased*) Barn Owl (*Tyto alba*). Uglamore was a Pure Guard sub-lieutenant serving under Nyra. He was not always comfortable following her orders and silently questioned the principle of *Tyto* superiority. His doubts led him into strange and dangerous territory, and to a destiny far nobler than any he could have imagined.

A Brief Glossary of Useful Words

bisshen: *v.* (*Krakish*) to speak

bonk: *adj.* the strongest, most energetic fires

botkin: *n.* special bag for transporting ice weapons

breaklight: *n.* the meal owls enjoy at the end of the night, just before the break of dawn

chaw: *n.* a small team of owls with a specific set of skills; chaws at the Great Ga'Hoole Tree include navigation, search-and-rescue, weather interpretation, colliering, tracking, Ga'Hoolology, and metals

chaw-chop: *v.* to drop an owl from his or her chaw for an indefinite period of time, which is very humiliating

churr: *v.* to laugh

collier: *n.* a carrier of coals

creelies: *n.* heebie-jeebies

Deep Gray: *n.* just before dawn, when the black has faded but the sun has not yet spilled even the first sliver of a ray over the horizon

dwenk: *v.* (of the moon) wane; a progressively smaller part of its visible surface illuminated, so that it appears to decrease in size

fire blink: *v.* when an owl becomes transfixed by the light of a raging fire and goes yeep

firesight: *n.* the ability to see events that take place in faraway places or in the future in flames

fleckasia: *n.* the collective effect of flecks on the owl brain and gizzard

flecks: *n.* the smallest bits of an ironlike metal considered more precious than gold, prized by the owls of St. Aggie's and the Pure Ones for its ability to interfere with an owl's navigation abilities

flint: *v.* to have value

flint mop: *n.* the Ga'Hoolian form of punishment; roughly means to do something to pay back for the value that had been taken away

fliv: *v.* to flirt

frink: *v.* a rude word that means to severely irritate, as in "it frinks me off"

frisen: *n.* (*Krakish*) friend

fryke: *exclamation.* (*Krakish*) command for "freeze"

Ga: *n.* great spirit

gadfeather: *n.* an owl who travels from one region to the next with no planned destination and no real home; known for their singing as well as their garish ways

gallgrot: *n.* gall, mettle

gazooling: *n.* the noisy chatter of young owls

give it a blow: *exclamation.* lighten up

gizzard: *n.* considered the second stomach in owls, often called the muscular stomach, it filters out indigestible items such as bone, fur, hair, feathers, and teeth; it compresses the indigestible parts into a pellet; also an invaluable emotional guide, an owl's most profound feelings are attributed to it

gizzlemia: *n.* a blankness of the gizzard, which leads to a malfunction of the brain

gizzuition: *n.* the ability to understand something immediately from the gizzard without the normal reasoning processes

glaumora: *n.* owl heaven

Glaux: *n.* owls' Higher Being

gleek: *v.* to goof off; mess around; act up; as in "gleeking about"

Glowworm: *n.* a particular kind of coal valued for its density of heat

gollymope: *n.* a depressed state or one in such a state

goodlight: *exclamation.* what owls say to one another just before going to sleep for the day

graymalkin: *n.* bad owl

grog tree: *n.* a tree where owls gather to drink and socialize

grot-ghot: *n.* (*Krakish*) native

gunden: *adj.* (*Krakish*) good

hagsfiend: *n.* demonlike bird from the time of legends, thought to be extinct; larger than most owls and having some characteristics of crows; believed to have powers of nachtmagen

hagsmire: *n.* owl hell

hireclaw: *n.* an owl who lives apart from other owls, not belonging to any particular kingdom, who hires him- or herself out for battles

Hoolespyrrs: *n.* swirling, deceptive winds over the Sea of Hoolemere

Hoolian: *n.* the common language of the Southern Kingdoms

hordo: *n.* (*Krakish*) snake

hordonphonk: *n.* (*Krakish*) supremely beautiful snake

hukla-hukla: *exclamation.* snake-speak for "young owls will be young owls"

issen: *n.* (*Krakish*) ice

issen blauen: *n.* (*Krakish*) blue ice, used to make goggles; also the goggles themselves

issen vintygg: *n.* (*Krakish*) deep ice

kerplonken: *adj.* (*Krakish*) all over; broken; useless

kraal: *n.* (*Krakish*) pirate

Krakish: *n.* the ancient language of the Northern Kingdoms

lochinvyrr: *n.* (*Krakish*) a code of honor between the hunter and the hunted

moon blink: *v.* to expose for long periods to the full shine of the moon, forcing owls' minds to become confused and incapable of making simple decisions; to destroy an owl's will and individual personality, making him or her perfectly obedient

mu: *n.* a very soft metal that blocks magnetic fields

nachtmagen: *n.* bad magic originating in the time of legends

new: *v.* (of the moon) wax; have a progressively larger part of its visible surface illuminated, so that it appears to increase in size

Nimsy Night: *n.* the festival held on the shortest night and longest day of the year

nooties: *n.* flavorful nuts that grow on the Great Ga'Hoole Trees during the time of the Copper-Rose Rain

owl stone event: *n.* an event of great significance in the development of a young owl

owlipoppen: *n.* little owl dolls made from down and molted feathers for chicks to lie with in the hollow; also used as decoys by the Guardians during the invasion of the canyonlands

pyte: *n.* a unit of measurement roughly equal to the wingspan of a Whiskered Screech

racdrops: *exclamation.* short for raccoon droppings; one of the worst curse words an owl can say

riffle: *v.* to ruffle one's feathers so as to accentuate the white spots (Spotted Owls only)

ryb: *n.* teacher

scroom: *n.* the disembodied spirit of an owl who has died but has not made his or her way to glaumora

scroomsaw: *n.* owl soul

shatter: *v.* to expose an owl to flecks under "certain conditions" that cause the owl to become massively disoriented and lose his or her sense of self; the gizzard becomes like a stone, and the owl becomes incapable of sorting out emotions and feelings, sometimes causing delusions

Short Light: *n.* in the Northern Kingdoms, the two days surrounding the longest night of the year, when the sun never rises more than the tiniest bit above the horizon

shred: *v.* to dart in and out of the edges of a fire, a colliering flight maneuver

skog: *n.* (*Krakish*) singer, storyteller

slipgizzle: *n.* owl spy, secret agent

sliptween: *n.* a nest-maid snake and member of the harp guild who leaps from one octave to another while playing the great grass harp

smee holes: *n.* natural steam vents in the Earth, found in the Northern Kingdoms

sprink: *v. and exclamation.* the worst owl curse word

spronk: *n.* forbidden knowledge

starsight: *n.* the ability to see the future in dreams

thronkenspeer: *n.* threat display

trufynkken: *adj.* (*Krakish*) drunk

turnfeather: *n.* owl traitor

turnscale: *n.* snake traitor

tween time: *n.* dusk; the time between the last drop of sun and the first shadows of the evening

tweener: *n.* the evening meal; the first food owls consume after waking

twixt time: *n.* dawn

wilf: *v.* when an owl becomes frightened and his or her feathers lie flat, making him or her seem smaller

williwaw: *n.* a sudden violent wind

yarp: *v.* to cough up a pellet

yarpie barpies: *n.* owl diarrhea

yeep: *adj.* when a bird loses its instincts to fly, its wings lock mid-flight, and it suddenly plummets to the ground, as in "going yeep"

yoiks: *adj.* crazy; loony; out of one's mind

Beyond the Beyond

Shadow Forest

Silverve

Southern
Kingdoms

The Barrer

Forest
Kingdor
of
Ambala

St. Aegolius Canyons

St. Aegolius Academy
for Orphaned Owls

N

Northern Kingdoms

Glauxian Brothers
Retreat

Bitter
Sea

Kiel Bay

Stormfast Island

Bay of Fangs

Everwinter Sea

Ice T

Ice
Narrows

Dark Fowl Island

Southern
Kingdoms